THE

HARLAXTON

HEIST

Linda E. Minton

Linda E. Minton

CONTENTS

CHARACTERS

Mrs. Clarke – local produce lady

Ella Cook – American aviator

Cubby and Maggie – British evacuees

Sergeant Mark Elderhurst – U.S. Army jeep driver

Ruth King – British cook

Lois Lovelace – Ella's American co-pilot

Lieutenant MacGregor – Agnes' superior officer

Sam Marlowe – Harlaxton gardener

Sarah Marlowe – Wife of Harlaxton gardener

Skye Marlowe – Barmaid at The Gregory

Bob Marshall – U.S. Army Air Corps Navigator

Mac McDonnell – airplane mechanic

Colonel Mills – Intelligence Officer

Vera Slaton Nuckols – U.S. Army cook

Cliff Ray – U.S Army airplane mechanic

Edie Slate – U.S. code breaker

Emily Smith – U. S. Army cook

General Stevens – Commander at Harlaxton

General Sullivan – Commander at High Wycombe

Agnes Taylor – U.S. Army cook

Midge Whitethorpe – British cook

WAAC Training Facility

Daytona Beach, Florida

December 1942

"The first WAAC (Women's Army Auxiliary Corps) recruits arrived in {WAAC Training Facility} October 1942, and eventually some 20,000 women received training at Daytona Beach. The recruits were housed initially in the Osceola Hotel and a local hospital, but additional buildings were soon leased or built by the military."

www.museumoffloridahistory.com

Chapter 1

Hauling their gear up to the Osceola Hotel, twenty-three-year old Agnes Taylor and another recruit, Vera Slaton, heard, "When your name is called, step forward and pick up your new gear. Get your bunk made and ready for roll call at 0900 hours. You are soldiers now and it's time to look like it! Agnes Taylor, pick up your uniform and deposit your civilian clothes to the right," barked Lieutenant MacGregor as she strutted down the hall.

"I'm not sure that I made the right choice picking the WAACs for my new life!" Red headed Agnes said to Vera, the dark-haired girl beside her.

"I know what you mean." Vera Slaton, short and slim, wrinkled her nose and headed to her new home with all the other girls. "I think I will take this comfy bunk by the window. Sure!" Vera said eyeing the lumpy mattress and narrow bed with disdain.

"I had to share a bedroom with two of my sisters, so this will be just like home with a lot of sisters. I think I will stretch out next to you," Agnes replied with a slight southern drawl.

Agnes remarked shortly, "Agnes Taylor from Tennessee - nice to meet you. My friends call me Aggie. It's been a long day of traveling. I had to get up early and travel a couple hours to board the train. I've never been to Florida or any place really. Where are you from?"

"I'm Vera Slaton from Hanson, Kentucky, so we are already neighbors. I thought I detected a Southern accent. It's nice to meet you too. I hope we get something to eat soon. I'm starving! That lieutenant is grouchy, don't you think? I guess they're not supposed to be our friends."

Agnes thought, the lieutenant reminds me of someone I used to know back home in Tennessee. Sometimes people really enjoy being the boss. I guess I will have to watch my attitude around her. This is the first time I have been away from home. I'm feeling a little homesick.

Looking away quickly from Vera, Agnes said. "I have twin sisters and a brother at home. When the guys around our small town of Red Boiling Springs, Tennessee, began enlisting and going off to war, I thought I should do something for the war effort too. I had been teaching some of the local kids, including my sisters, in a one room school for a couple years after I graduated from high school."

"It will take me some time to get used to being around so many people and having to take orders. My father died when I was very young, and my mother remarried a man who didn't like children. So, my grandmother raised me until I left home. My grandmother was not very happy to see me sign up," sighed Vera. "My boyfriend, Chester, was especially upset with me. He doesn't think girls should be in the military. I suppose he'll get over it."

"It seems as though not many mothers like to see their girls go so far away from home. Vera, what do you think about the Army so far?"

"As you know, in the South we are very patriotic. All the boys in my high school enlisted as soon as they could. Many of them didn't wait to finish high school. So, I thought I would do my part by giving blood; however, I didn't weigh enough to give blood!" Vera informed Agnes. "As you can see, I'm not very big...but I was big enough to join up!" The two girls laughed together at Vera's comment and continued organizing and putting away their gear.

"I have heard from some of the girls that the guys are not always keen to have women in the military. I personally haven't had any problems with the men, but I guess it is more of a feeling; they think we should be at home with the children and not in the military like they are. I suppose we will just have to show them we belong," Vera said proudly.

Agnes smoothed her hands over her uniform and thought, I agree with Vera, I think we are going to be great friends. I want to be a cook. I have been cooking since I was old enough to reach the stove. It's a great way to help with the war.

"Aggie, since you're tall and slim, we are certainly going to look different cooking together. Maybe, we will be a good compliment to each other. Do you have a special boyfriend back home?"

Agnes pondered Vera's question carefully for a few minutes before she answered. Slowly, she responded to Vera's question, "I did have, a guy who I dated for a long time, but things didn't work out between us. So, no one special back home."

Agnes thought, I wish there were still a special guy that I enjoyed spending time with when I was growing up. Her thoughts always seem to come back to Cliff. Maybe that could change – time will tell.

The next week ~

Agnes started to stir as all the girls in the unit were talking and going to the showers. All the women in the unit were a lot of fun. Most of them followed the rules about being out late at night. "Hey, everyone let's do short showers today. Yesterday, the water was cold by the time I hit the showers." Someone across the room shouted, "You better get up earlier, Taylor, if you want a warm shower around here."

Looking over at the still sleeping Vera, Agnes gave her friend a shake, "Hey, Vera, get up! It's 0530 hours, and we have reveille at 0600 hours. Today, is our first day of food classes and then it's marching, always, marching! Did you look through the "Army Food and Messing" book we were given yesterday about food management? It has some recipes and suggestions about how to set up the mess kitchen as well as Army regulations about food. You know the old saying, 'An army marches on its stomach'; well it's our job to see that our guys and gals are fed well, and we take our position seriously."

Laughing at Agnes, Vera replied, "Golly, you sure listened in class. Hey, I'm just teasing you...we do have an important job to do."

"I know, Vera. I have always cooked for the family, but cooking for hundreds of people is different, of course. I'll just do my best and hope I don't poison anyone!" Agnes teased Vera back.

"The military has been a challenge for me foodwise; as you have probably noticed, I'm a picky eater. My grandmother let me eat whatever I wanted or in other words, I didn't have to eat what I didn't want – like gravy. I don't like gravy on anything." Vera replied with a scowl on her face.

"Well, Vera, I hope you don't lose too much weight as the Army really doesn't care what you like to eat, I have noticed. Our family didn't have a lot of money, so we ate whatever food was put on the table."

"Okay, I will survive the food thing...I really enjoy the Army and am making a lot of new friends. I'll sure miss you when you ship out. Hey, we better get a move on. Speaking of food – I hope we have something good for dinner – without gravy on it!"

Vera thought, at least when I am making the menus, I can make decisions about what food is served. It will be a good adventure in the weeks ahead.

Agnes laughed at Vera and gathered her personal laundry to take to the laundry room. Just like at home, she had to use a laundry tub and wash board to scrub her underwear clean. The girls could send out their uniforms to be cleaned and pressed, but their personal items were done by them...no pampering for the WACs.

Six weeks later ~

The girls had been through basic training and were getting ready to go in different directions now. After chores and preparations for tomorrow were finished, the girls decided to play some rummy before turning in for the night. Since they had to get up so early, there weren't many late nights anymore. Vera won at cards and some of the girls were coming back to the barracks after playing some baseball to relax.

Agnes thought she would get some sleep, "Hey, Vera, turn that light off. You know there are nighttime black outs since they spotted those German U-boats off the coast of Jacksonville Beach in April. We don't want to give the Germans a target to aim for, now do we?"

"No, I'm sure we don't," Vera grimaced and quickly turned off the light as Agnes had requested.

It was reported there were spies who came ashore near Ponte Vedra Beach. Then, they boarded a bus for Jacksonville, Florida, and were planning lots of terrible things, but they were eventually discovered and arrested.

"Well, changing the gruesome subject of spies, I've signed up for Cooks and Bakers School which will last for two weeks. Now, I just want to take off these shoes and rest my feet! What are you going to do after Basic Training, Vera?" Agnes sighed and sat down on her bunk.

"I'm going to Cooks and Bakers School too. Then I am going to Mess Sergeant's School. I will spend four weeks here, and then it's on to Stuttgart, Arkansas, after Mess Sergeant School. Why don't you try that too? You would be great at being in charge."

"Are you saying I'm bossy! What a buddy you are, Vera."

"Did you know that Stuttgart, Arkansas, is the duck hunting capital of the world?" Vera replied proudly.

"Is that right. Well, I am sure glad I'm going to miss that. I signed up to go to England. I know someone who is stationed over there. I have never been overseas, so it will be an adventure, I think."

"Sure, it will be. I wish I could go with you, but my boyfriend, Chester, would have a fit! He wants to get married, but I want to go on to study some more. I would love to be a dietician since I know a lot about food."

Vera and Agnes decided to go to Cooks and Bakers School. They were being sent to Fort Dix, New Jersey for Cooks and Bakers School which wasn't far from New York City. Agnes would love to go to a big city while she's in the service.

"Hey, Vera, you know Emily Smith, don't you?   Well, she wants to enjoy the sights in New York City before we shove off. We have a two-day pass before we board the ship for England. Do you want to go with us? You can get a troop train to Arkansas the next morning."

"Sure, Agnes, that sounds swell to me! I haven't been to New York City. I want to go to Ellis Island, the Empire State Building, and ..."

"Whoa, Vera, we are only there for one day, not a week. We will do what we can to get all that in. I want to see all those things, plus go to a Broadway show.   That's something I have read about and, hopefully, it will be possible. I'll check with Emily to see what she thinks. She is from Brooklyn and knows the ins and outs of getting around the city. We can depend on her to help us out."

"I'm going to miss swimming in the warm blue ocean and lying on the beach when we have liberty," Vera said sadly.

The girls have one more day of marching and inspection on the beach. They will line up with the jeeps and stand inspection tomorrow morning at 0600. Then, Tuesday is the day they leave the sandy beaches and warm weather in beautiful Florida to go to their next assignment, Ft. Dix, New Jersey.

"Hey, we can plan our girls' trip to the big busy city of New York. I'm up for an adventure!" Agnes replied with a huge grin on her face. The three girls decided on a hotel and some of the places on Vera's list. Agnes was just happy they might get to a Broadway show. Emily was always up for a swell time.

The Next Day ~

0600 hours

"Rise and shine, Vera. We only have fifteen minutes to get some chow and out to the beach for inspection. You better get going. I'll see you on the beach." Agnes told Vera as she put on her hat, gave her hair one final look, and hurriedly left for breakfast.

Once she arrived at the beach, she took her position along with the other girls. Agnes found her place as the girls sang a familiar WAAC song and marched in unison down the packed sand of the famous Daytona Beach.

We're the Women's Army Corps

From the East to the West we're the bestest

of the best

We're the Women's Army Corps

So it hail all hail

The women will not fail

To help make the foe turn tail

Join our song and with us march along

In the Women's Army Corps

Agnes thought to herself; I'm proud I decided to become a WAAC and leave home. It wasn't easy to do. I do miss my family, but this won't last forever. I get to see the world in addition to serving my country. I'll write another letter tonight and let mom and the family know what I have been doing in Florida and when I will be shipping out to England.

Agnes didn't know what to expect when she signed up to be a WAAC. The recruitment poster made it look exciting. She hoped to see the world. She looked at the perfect rows of American girls who were doing exactly what she was doing. The girls sang loudly and proudly.

Taking a quick look over her shoulder, Agnes smiled to see Vera had made it in time. She thought to herself; I'm going to miss Vera and the wonderful sandy beach of Daytona, but it's time to move on to another chapter in my life.

Farther down the line, Emily Smith was marching with the other girls in her row. It was difficult for Emily to keep her thoughts on what was going on in front of her. In her mind, she kept rereading the letter she received about her high school friend in Brooklyn. Michael Crenstein, a boy she dated from her neighborhood, was missing. He enlisted right after the attack on Pearl Harbor when war was declared.

She couldn't get it out of her mind. It was against regs to go into town and make phone calls. Maybe her mother could give her some information about Michael. She had to know before she shipped out to England. Where was he captured or killed? How is his family? Why did she quit her job at the bank to join the Army? All these questions were swimming in her head.

A plan began to form in her mind. Maybe she could pull this off and not get into too much trouble. Time would tell...

After most of the girls were in the barracks for the evening, Emily slipped out the side door and walked through an unguarded open gate. It was a brisk twenty-minute walk into town to the drugstore. She could use the pay phone quickly and be back before she was missed. Her plan had to work.

Emily, always the one who bent the rules, slipped into the drugstore and looked to see if the phone booth was empty. Fortunately, the phone was not being used, and she could step inside and make her call. Her mother picked up on the second ring and accepted the charges for the call.

"Hello, Mom. I received your letter about Michael. I was so worried about him; I had to call and see what else you know about his situation."

"Well, Emily, I'm afraid I don't know anything else I can tell you. Are you okay?"

"Sure Mom, I'm fine. I'm leaving tomorrow for England. I'll write whenever I can. Tell Dad I miss him too. I need to go now. Love you." Emily hung up the phone and looked into the eyes of the MPs coming her way.

Oh no! I have really messed up now, she thought dreading what was coming next. The MPs took her arm and guided her out of the drugstore. They asked if she had a pass to be in town at this hour. Of course, she hadn't thought of asking for a pass for this emergency – in her mind.

"No, sir. I don't have a pass."

"Come with us." They escorted Emily back to base and dropped her off at Lieutenant MacGregor's office.

Lieutenant MacGregor looked at Emily and shook her head. Emily was a bright girl, but always seemed to make the wrong choice.

After the MPs left, Lieutenant MacGregor said, "Okay, Private Smith, what do you have to say for yourself?"

Knowing she should be honest about what happened tonight, she said, "Well, Lieutenant MacGregor, I received a letter with some disturbing news about a fella I was dating before I enlisted. I wanted to know if my mother knew any more about his situation. I didn't think about getting permission before I left camp. Honestly, sometimes I just don't think before I act, I guess."

"Private Smith, you do know you will be sailing oversea in a few days, don't you?"

"Yes. At least, I hope I'm still going with the other girls. Please give me another chance to do some good for the Army. I was just so upset I didn't make a very good decision. I realize that now."

"Well, I hope so. Private Smith, you are a very intelligent young woman. I am going to overlook tonight's mistake and hope you have learned your lesson. If you were in a combat situation, the consequences could have been very different for you and your fellow soldiers. Think before you act, private."

"Yes, I will. Thank you, Lieutenant MacGregor."

"Go back to your barrack now."

Emily walked back to her barracks and changed her clothes in the dark. She didn't want to awaken everyone. She slipped into her bunk quietly and thought how lucky she had been tonight. Lieutenant MacGregor did have a heart after all. She said a prayer for Michael - wherever he was now.

New York City, New York

April 1943

"WAAC was established for the purpose of making available to the national defense the knowledge, skill, and special training of women of the nation."

Chapter 2

Early the next day, the girls boarded a train to New York City to begin the fun of exploring a large exciting city. Emily was a little subdued after her escape yesterday. She wasn't going to share her evening conversation with Lieutenant MacGregor with the girls. Today was going to be all about good times.

Agnes Taylor looked up at the bright lights and tall buildings of Times Square and thought how far away she was from Red Boiling Springs, Tennessee.

"I thought signing up to be a WAAC seemed like the patriotic thing to do. It was sure hard to leave the family right before Christmas. Times are tough and there was never a lot of presents under that scraggly pine tree my twin sisters, Alice and Alene, and I cut down before I left," Agnes said sadly to Vera.

Vera replied to Agnes sympathetically, "As bad or sad as we think things might be for us, we need to remember the men who are fighting in the trenches and in the

Pacific. Now, that is really a difficult time. Many of them haven't been home since they enlisted. We just have to do our jobs, always remembering every job in the military is important."

"Gosh, Vera, you sound like Uncle Sam! You could be a recruiter or something! Hey, I'm teasing of course. It's just tough to leave family at home and come to a very different place. However, I love New York City."

"Girls, it has been a terrific day. I can't believe we have been to the Empire State Building, ridden the Staten Island Ferry to see the Statue of Liberty, and Times Square all in one day! What was your favorite thing we saw today, Vera?" Agnes asker her friend.

"Oh Aggie, it was all just wonderful. I guess my favorite was the Empire State Building. I have heard about it all my life...never dreaming I would actually get to see all this." As Vera pointed to the tall buildings of the city. "Thanks, for including me in this adventure before we all are sent to different areas of the world."

Vera and Agnes heard their friend calling for them from across the room. "Hey, Taylor and Slaton, you are going to make us late staring at everything. Get over here and get some food before we take in a show around 2000 hours," Emily shouted in her distinctive Brooklyn accent. Emily was very familiar with this area having grown up in Brooklyn. Her parents were not very happy to see Emily sign up and go off to war, especially since she was leaving the United States and going to England.

"Well, Emily, this is old hat to you since you grew up around here. I've never seen a building over two stories in my life. There aren't any subways or trains where I grew up. This is wonderful!" Vera said.

"New York City is never old hat to me. It's a wonderful exciting city! I'm looking forward to showing you girls around my part of the world. Come on, let's get this show on the road," Emily explained to Vera and Agnes.

"Okay, bright eyes, you have to take in some nourishment, or you will faint dead away before we get on the ship tomorrow for England. Servicemen don't like their cooks to be too skinny. It makes the men nervous that their food isn't any good. We must keep up the morale in this war! Here, eat a ham sandwich. It will put meat on those skinny bones," laughed feisty Emily as she kidded Agnes.

"What show are we going to see tonight?" Vera shouted over the loud music playing on stage of the restaurant.

"I heard that the Ziegfeld Follies was a big hit. It may be hard to get tickets though," replied Emily.

Vera said, "I have always heard about the Radio City Rockettes. They are supposed to be fantastic to watch. The girls are beautiful, and they have wonderful costumes! Are they performing now?"

"Gee, I don't know if they are or not, but..." replied Emily.

As the waitress approached their table, she said loudly, "Hey, girls, Oklahoma is opening today at the St. James Theatre. It is supposed to be swell. It's a musical with lots of singing and dancing. I'm sure you would enjoy it. Why don't you give it a try?"

Agnes was eager for some big city entertainment and the waitress' recommendation was surely appreciated. What better advice than someone who lived and worked in New York. "Sounds like the ticket to me...if we can get a ticket," laughed everyone. "Let's go, girls."

The girls pooled their money and paid the bill. Getting up to leave the restaurant, Agnes thought, well, let's try. You never know what will happen. Goodness knows we are used to marching and standing around in the military.

Emily was the unofficial leader of the group. Agnes was so excited to see a big city that she couldn't help gawking at the strange sights as they walked the ten blocks to the theater. Upon arriving at the theater, "Oh no, we'll never get seats tonight! The line is wrapped around the building," Vera exclaimed sadly.

After about thirty minutes, the theater manager came out and took all the service people out of the line. After all the servicemen and women were inside the theater, the manager said, "We have special seats for the military. Follow me, please." They all followed the man in charge, as they were used to doing.

Emily, Vera, and Agnes found their seats in the third row in the center section. "These seats are fabulous!" gushed Vera. The usher came over and said, "Madam, are these seats agreeable for you? We want your night to be special." He smiled broadly and gave them each a program for the show. "They are lovely, thanks," Agnes said graciously.

Emily leaned over and said to Agnes, "I have never had seats this good before. This is going to be a fabulous evening, girls."

Agnes replied, "I've never been to a show before! I would have been happy with the back row of the balcony."

"Quiet, Aggie, they could move us there yet!" joked Vera and Emily together.

"No, it's wonderful to know that New York City values us and what we do for the war effort," Emily beamed.

The lights dimmed, and the lush red curtain started to rise. This was going to be the beginning of many firsts in my life in the WAAC thought Agnes.

After the show was over and the girls were walking out of the theater, Agnes remarked to Vera and Emily, "Emily, that was the most wonderful thing I have ever seen!"

Agnes loved the music and all the stunning costumes. This had been a great way for the girls to share something special before they went their separate ways. They had been together for the past couple months with their training, so it was going to be sad to leave some of the girls behind. In the military, there is a special bond among fellow soldiers.

"We have an early morning, so I guess we had better get back to our hotel. Don't you think, girls?" Agnes remarked.

"I suppose you are right, Agnes." Both girls agreed with Agnes reluctantly. "I just hate to go to sleep and miss anything," Vera said.

Emily was reluctant to pass up a good time and convinced the girls to stay up a while longer. "Come on, girls. I think we have time to get a cup of coffee before we turn in. There is a cute little Italian coffee shop, *The Peabody*, down the street that is open all night. Sounds like a brilliant idea to me."

Vera thought it sounded like a great idea, and said, "Do they have good apple pie? I would love a piece of hot apple pie and vanilla ice cream...I'm always hungry"

"Oh Vera, you're always ready for dessert, but apple pie does sound like the ticket. I guess I'm not sleepy now." Emily replied.

"Okay Emily – show us the coffee and pie," Agnes grinned and followed the girls down the busy New York sidewalk to the café`. She could spend a week here and not get tired of seeing this large bustling city.

Finding a booth, Emily slid into a seat and picked up the menu. "I don't know why I'm picking up a menu when I know I'm getting the apple pie and coffee. I bet it's not as good as what you make Agnes. You can certainly cook! A man would be crazy not to marry you for your cooking alone, not to mention you are such a sweetheart."

Agnes blushed bright red and smiled at her best buddies. She wasn't used to such sweet compliments, especially after going through boot camp. The lieutenant had been ruthless and demanding to the girls.

"Oh, come on Emily. Agnes is nice, but don't pile on the compliments … she's not going to buy pie for all of us! Are you Agnes?"

"Well, I would have if I had thought to bring more money. I sent home most of my money already. The lieutenant said we wouldn't need money where we were going."

Vera grinned and said, "I was just teasing…I'm treating everyone. I am the one who's staying in the United States while you two may be sailing away into danger. You never know what will happen on the open sea on the way to England. So, this is my bon voyage gift to you both and thanks for inviting me on this adventure to New York City."

Then the waitress appeared, and the trio ordered apple pie and coffee. When the waitress left the table, Emily said, "This was an excellent idea. Maybe we will just stay up all night! What do you say girls?" Emily giggled.

"Oh, Emily, you are such a crazy girl," Aggie said.

"Vera, you will need your beauty sleep before you go to Arkansas and meet the duck hunters."

"Girls, I heard that women aren't allowed off the base during duck hunting season. So, no danger of getting shot or meeting the duck hunters."

The waitress returned with three slices of warm apple pie and hot coffee for each of them. Although the sweet apple pie, which smelled of cinnamon, was delicious, it was not as good as Agnes' cobblers. They made a toast to come back to New York City after the war was over.

"Hopefully, it's soon!" Vera replied happily lifting her coffee mug up high and giving the girls a huge grin.

The next morning ~

"Vera, we are going to miss you," said Emily and Agnes. Vera picked up her duffle bag and heaved it over her small shoulders. Shaking her head, Vera said again, "I'm going to Stuttgart, Arkansas. Who has ever heard of that place before? While I get to head the kitchen there, I will be thinking of you two going overseas and all the adventures you are going to have. Make sure you write and let me know what is going on in England. Try not to embarrass the WAACs while you are there, girls!"

Emily and Agnes nodded their still sleepy heads and smiled broadly. They had a wonderful time last night, but the trio didn't get much sleep.

"What time do you catch your train to Arkansas?" asked Agnes sadly. "Emily and I are leaving on the Queen Mary at 0700 hours. It is a fast ship, and we don't have a convoy because it can outrun the German U-boats."

Thinking how dangerous that sounded, Vera said, "That's wonderful, Agnes. My train leaves for Arkansas soon, so I'll say goodbye for now. Remember the promise we made last night to get together after the war ends. We will have a victory dinner in New York City to celebrate beating the enemies."

"It's a deal," said both Emily and Agnes together. After giving Vera a tight hug, Agnes said, "We'll write as soon as we are settled at High Wycombe, I promise," shouted Emily over the sound of the arriving troop train.

The train was crowded with soldiers and a few civilians tucked in here and there. Some of the GIs were hanging out the train windows waving and whistling at the girls standing on the train platform. The girls laughed at the men's antics and gave each other one more last hug.

"Emily, I am really going to miss Vera. She is a firecracker and will be a great Mess Sergeant. She encouraged me to go to Mess Sergeant school. Well, we better get to the train before we are left behind. Goodbye, New York!" Agnes replied as she and Emily ran to catch the train to the dock.

~~~~~~~~

Vera had heard about the camp in Stuttgart. There was an orientation meeting for the girls going to the Stuttgart Army Air Field. The girls were told there would be German and Italian POWs at the camp. The prisoners would be required to work on the base. Some of them might be working in her Mess Hall. She didn't know how she felt about having the enemy so close to her. The Mess Hall had not been built long, and she and her staff would be responsible for setting up the kitchen.

Life was going to be different for her in the coming weeks. She was going to miss Agnes and Emily desperately. They had become great friends after their adventures in New York City. She almost wished she had signed up to go to England too. Boy, would Chester be angry if she went overseas! Oh well, she would make the best of Stuttgart and the duck hunters.

~~~~~~~~

Upon arriving at the dock, Agnes carried her duffle and hat on the way to meet the rest of her unit. "Hey, Emily, ready to join everyone? I am so excited to be going to England. My family said this is a chance of a lifetime to get to travel and see the world. Unfortunately, there is some danger involved in getting to England."

"Well, I hear the British ship Queen Mary is one of the best troop transports around. Even though we don't have a convoy to protect us, I feel good about our chances."

"Honestly, Emily. You don't worry about anything! Don't you know the large ship makes a bigger target for the Germans! I want to help the U.S. win this war!" said Agnes proudly.

Agnes had read about the Battle of Britain in 1940 which occurred before the United States had gotten involved in the war. The Germans were attacking the British airfields and destroying their Spitfires. The Germans bombed London causing much devastation - damage to buildings and death of civilians. The English people had suffered extremely in the years since Adolph Hitler's reign of terror had begun.

~~~~~~~~

Aboard the Queen Mary~

"Aggie, are we ever going to get to England?"

"Well, Emily, there is a war on, and the ship has to be careful of German U-boats. Remember, we were told the voyage should take about a week's time. I'm sure it won't be long now. I agree those calisthenics first thing in the morning are getting plenty old."

"Yes, and so is KP. Uh oh, Aggie. I see Lieutenant MacGregor coming this way, and she doesn't look happy. I feel like I need to apologize every time I see her."

"Maybe if you didn't push the rules so much you wouldn't have that feeling. Did that ever occur to you?"

Lieutenant MacGregor stopped in front of the girls and asked Emily to follow her to her office. Aggie gave Emily a sympathetic look and walked back to her room below deck. Emily was correct about one thing; she would be happy to be on dry ground too.

Emily entered Lieutenant MacGregor's temporary office aboard the ship. It was about as stern looking as the woman who occupied it.

"Private Smith, I have reports you are hanging your personal laundry on the outside deck to dry. Is there any truth to the rumor?"

"Well, yes there could be some truth there. My laundry doesn't dry very well in my room. No one wants to wear wet undies."

"Are you aware there are hundreds of male soldiers and sailors on this ship?"

"Sure, I would have to be blind not to notice all the men, lieutenant." She thought of some of the guys looking at her curvy shape as she walked down the deck for the past week.

Lieutenant MacGregor put her hand up to hide a smile, but replied, "It's distracting to the men to see women's underwear flapping in the breeze. Do you understand what I am saying, private?"

"Yes, I do understand. I'll remove my laundry. It won't happen again."

"See that it doesn't. You are dismissed now."

"As punishment, you have two more days of KP for choosing your own method of drying your laundry."

Emily closed the door and went to collect her laundry from its temporary drying place. As she approached her private drying area, she found it wasn't so private. There were a group of sailors gazing at her underwear. When would she ever learn! She snatched up the undies and hurried back to her bunk.

Two more days of KP! She hated KP. She was sure she wouldn't get any sympathy from Aggie. Aggie was such a rule follower!

The RMS *Queen Mary*, named after the wife of King George V, was scheduled to dock at Southhampton in the next couple days. Since the war started, the *Queen Mary* had been converted into a troopship to transport men and women to where they were needed. Some of the rules aboard ship were no swearing, no obscene or profane language, and no gambling. The GIs chose not to observe the gambling ban.

After the ship docked and troops were dispersed to different locations, Emily and Agnes boarded a train to London. After arriving in London, the girls climbed into trucks for the trip to High Wycombe along with other GIs who were stationed at the base.

High Wycombe, England

Forty miles west of London

May 1943

There was a lot to know about this historic base, but the Eighth Air Force Bomber Command incorporated Camp Lynn which was named in honor of Second Lieutenant Lynn who didn't return from a raid July 4, 1942. Also, Daws Hill is an underground bunker located underneath Roundabout Hill. There may be many secrets in this place.

Chapter 3

I wonder if Cliff will be happy to see me after all this time and remember the happy times we had in high school. It's funny how your circumstances change. This war has changed my life thought Agnes.

As the truck pulled up to the base, Agnes said to Emily, "One of the girls just told me this was a large girls' school, Wycombe Abbey School, before it was commandeered for the RAF or Royal Air Force. Isn't it impressive: A three-story tall brick building and these beautiful grounds - lovely flower gardens, a nice lake, and hedges. This looks like a vacation area instead of a military base. How did we get so lucky, Emily?"

"I don't know Aggie. Do you know where we are staying? It's beautiful here. Lush green rolling hills – lovely!"

Emily looking over the beautiful landscape said, "I don't know where we are assigned to stay. Where is Lieutenant MacGregor? She said to stow our things near Barracks A. I would like to look over the Mess Hall this afternoon," replied Emily.

"Sure, that would be great. I hope we are well-stocked and don't have to make a run to the commissary today. When do we start cooking?"

"I don't know, Aggie, but there is a good-looking fella coming toward us. No, looks like he's looking at *you!* Do you know him?"

Tall, slender and smiling broadly, Cliff Ray approached the girls, "Aggie, I can't believe it's you! What are you doing here?" said the dark-haired man standing before her.

Those familiar loving feelings were still there when she heard Cliff's voice. Looking up at Cliff, Agnes replied pleasantly, "I joined up after you left. Your mom said you were stationed here, so I thought why not come say hello to a fellow Tennessean. Besides I thought I should do something for the war effort too. I couldn't let you go and fight the war without me!"

"Well, you could have knocked me over with a feather when I saw you get out of that truck. It's been nearly two years since I saw you. I guess a hello hug is allowed in the Army," Cliff replied while reaching over and gently hugging Agnes. Cliff remembered how wonderful it was to be with Aggie. She was still special to him.

"Excuse me, if you two want to be alone with this reunion business...." squeaked Emily.

"Oh no, sorry Emily! I guess we just got carried away...not seeing each other for a while," Aggie said slightly embarrassed.

"Cliff, this is Emily Smith. Emily and I are assigned to the Mess Hall here at High Wycombe. We need to find our barracks and check in with Lieutenant MacGregor by 1400 hours. I'm sure I'll see you around. It's really swell to see you."

"I'm sure you will – and soon too." Grinning Cliff ran back to the hangar where he kept the B-29s running smoothly.

Looking after Cliff, Agnes said, "Emily, let's get our duffle bags and find the other gals. Hey, is this your bag? I don't remember seeing it here before, do you?"

"No, wonder what's inside..." said Emily as she reached for the strange bag. Aggie knew the bag was an Escape Kit. She had seen pictures of them in an old manual in the barrack. Also, some of the girls had mentioned their boyfriends talking about them.

Before she could open the bag, the girls heard a loud voice say, "Taylor, Smith – fall in. Get your gear and report to the Mess Hall – now! We need to inventory supplies and get acquainted with the RAF staff that are already here," shouted Lieutenant MacGregor.

As Lieutenant MacGregor walked away, Emily replied, "Lieutenant MacGregor, we have a bag that doesn't belong..."

"Forget it, Smith. They need Taylor and you over at the Mess Hall now! March!" said Lt. MacGregor angrily. "Clear this area!"

Agnes and Emily didn't wait around for any more trouble from Lieutenant MacGregor. They quickly secured their belongings and hightailed it over to the Mess Hall.

After the girls found the Mess Hall, Agnes told the RAF staff, "I'm Corporal Taylor reporting for duty. I will be the Mess Sergeant and Private Smith does the baking. So, she will be checking to see if there is flour and other baking supplies that she might need."

"Delighted to see you girls, I'm Midge Whitethorpe and this is Ruth King. We are both with the RAF, and we need some help right away." There were about 1500 American soldiers here, plus the RAF pilots and staff. We have a lot of service people to feed. There were women doing lots of jobs, from compiling weather reports, maintaining aircraft, serving on airfields, cooking, or working in Intelligence and the motor pool.

Midge went on to say, "When you go for supplies, merchants will try to shove that bloody lamb off on you when they can but see if they have some beef if possible. The guys like it so much better. Also, the powdered milk and eggs are fairly tasteless, but we have to serve them anyway," said Midge wrinkling her nose.

"Oh, by the way," she stated, "I've been here for about eighteen months. It's a real nice assignment. There's always something going on here."

"Thanks for the information, Midge. I'll call the motor pool after we inspect the kitchen and inventory the supplies," replied Agnes.

Walking into the large clean kitchen, Agnes looked around at the ample supplies and the adequate cooking and baking equipment. She thought, the kitchen looked good and there shouldn't be any problem getting meals prepared here. "Midge, what's that barking?"

"Oh, well...I know it's against regs, but we found, or rather he found us, this cute little dog hanging around the back door a few days ago. He's a dachshund and just as cute as can be! We try to keep him quiet, so we won't get into trouble, but sometimes he has other ideas!" When the pantry door was opened, out bounced out a wild blur of black and brown fur. "Oh my, he is great! Oh, only one problem! He's a German!!" Everyone laughed and petted the wild little dog.

Emily asked Midge, "What's his name?"

Midge thought for a few minutes; she really hadn't thought about a name for the dog. She just hoped he would be claimed by someone soon, so he didn't need a name to be cared for and fed. "Since you're my partners in crime, what do you two think?"

"Well, what about Frankie? You know since he is long and skinny like a frankfurter. I think that would be a wonderful name for him. You all agree?" Emily replied suddenly.

Aggie and Midge laughed and said, "He seems to like his name."

The dog was wagging his tail and licking Agnes' hand. He needs a good home, and he is so sweet, thought Midge. "What do you say, Agnes? Please!"

Agnes couldn't say no when the girls were so taken with the little dog. She thought it might be nice to have him around here too. Remembering all the pets around the farm, she replied cheerfully, "Okay, it's Frankie then. I guess we better get him something to eat before he eats my hand."

Midge brought some sausages out of the large upright cooler and cut them up for Frankie. She guessed, that should take care of him for a while. Apparently, he hasn't been fed for some time. I don't know if he belongs to anyone around here. No one has asked about him, and we can't just turn him out....

Agnes asked puzzled, "Where does he sleep when we're all gone? How long has he been here?" Questions tumbled out as Agnes tried to look at the Frankie situation sensibly.

"Well, he has been sleeping under the prep table over in the corner of the kitchen for about a week. So far, no one has noticed him, or if they have, they haven't said a word about it. He is so sweet! It's nice to have a friendly face around here sometimes." Midge smiled down at Frankie and gave his ears a rub. Frankie rewarded Midge will a vigorous wag of his tail thumping on the kitchen floor.

I guess we'll have to keep him stowed in the corner away from our superiors. Trying to explain why there was a dog in a military kitchen might be a problem. She didn't want to get off on the wrong foot on her first assignment.

"Okay, I'll go over to the motor pool and to the commissary for supplies. Anyone have any requests for dinner tomorrow? Midge, I am assuming you have today's menu already planned," Agnes said to Midge.

Slim and petite Midge walked to the desk and pulled out a list of items needed to replenish the supply closet. She told Agnes to feel free to add anything that she wanted to the supply list. Americans surely prepare things differently than the British do. "The American guys will enjoy your cooking now. Any questions, girls?"

"No, looks like you run an efficient kitchen. I do have some recipes that I would like to try though. I'll pick up the supplies that I need while I am at the commissary."

Agnes looked over the list quickly and told Emily to look around and get accustomed to the kitchen layout and help Midge get things prepared for the next meal.

"Agnes, we will get acquainted and try to keep Frankie out of trouble. See you soon," Emily replied.

Agnes picked up Frankie and scratched behind his ears. "Goodbye, Frankie. Stay out of trouble." she whispered to the frisky little dog, thinking to herself, keeping this dog may be a big mistake! I really don't want to get attached to another male.

Later that evening~

Agnes lay in her bed watching the searchlights light up the dark sky over the base. The military had to be ever vigilant in watching for German planes. The Nazis were still a very strong force, and they could do a lot of damage to the planes and the airstrip. She thought of the various events of the day and her family at home. Life was going to be very different in the next few months in a foreign country. Aggie was hopeful she could make new friends and perhaps get closer to some old ones. Time would tell, she mused as she drifted off to sleep. Tomorrow would be a busy day...

Cliff's A Hero

High Wycombe, England

May 1943

"Bomber Command directly contributed to the attacks in the aircraft industry in Schweinfurt Germany." American bombers made hits on the airplane factories to keep the skies free from Luftwaffe attacks.

Chapter 4

Stuttgart and Dusseldorf, Germany, were almost completely destroyed due to Allied bombing. RAF bombers and American bombers took part in many raids on the cities. Dusseldorf was nearly left a heap of rubble. The Bosch factory in Stuttgart produced components for the Luftwaffe. Unfortunately, many civilians were killed in these raids. It has been reported that the factories which produced parts for the planes and armaments had forced labor working for the Nazis.

~~~~~~~~

Cliff arrived at the hangar early and ready for a busy day after the most recent skirmish which damaged many of the British planes. "Hey, has anyone seen Mac this morning? I wanted to ask his advice on a problem I've been having with this plane."

Several of the guys said they had not seen him yet. Cliff thought that was odd as he was always prompt. He was starting to worry about his friend, wondering where he could be. Has he been captured by the enemy? Is he hurt and can't come to work? No, this is a military base, and he can't be missing. Cliff's questions were answered soon.

After about an hour, Mac arrived, "Hello, Cliff, sorry I'm late, but I had sentry duty last night and was just relieved a few minutes ago."

Glad to see his friend was safe, he gave a sigh of relief and replied, "I knew it had to be something since you are always on time for work. What happened?"

"Well, you know there was a downed German plane over on the west field yesterday. I had to guard it during the night. There was this officer who wanted to get closer, but he didn't have his papers on him. So, I wouldn't let him pass. He got heated over the incident, and I had to go to HQ to explain my actions. All is clear now. Headquarters said I did the correct thing and reprimanded the officer...how about that?" Mac laughed easily.

"What do you need, Cliff?"

"I need some of your small crescent wrenches."

"I'll get my tools and be back to help you with this plane." Mac moved off to get his tools, leaving Cliff to study his problem.

Meanwhile, walking into the airfield hangar, Major Poole looked around for his favorite mechanic. Finding Sergeant Cliff Ray bent over an engine, he said, "Cliff, I want you to look at my plane. The engine sounds funny. Would you check it over? See what you think."

"Sure, Sir, I'd be happy to give it a look. What kind of sound does it make?"

"Well, it's difficult to describe exactly – a sort of whine, not the usual whir, I suppose...I'm not sure, but my gut says it's not right."

"When does it make this sound?"

Major Poole looked pensive then replied, "It makes the sound when I am banking to the right."

"Hmmm. That gives me some idea of what you are thinking, but I would like to go up with you so I can hear exactly what you're hearing. If that is okay, I will try to schedule it for today. Is that agreeable with you, sir? It's due for mandatory maintenance anyway."

"Sure, Cliff, that will be great. I'm eager to find the problem before I have to go up again."

After scheduling a maintenance and check-up flight plan with HQ, Cliff and Major Poole took his plane, *Tennessee Lady*, up for a check on the mysterious sound.

Later that day~

Now, that Cliff had heard the sound, he tore down the major's plane engine, a P-47 Thunderbolt, and looked over the parts carefully. While inspecting the engine parts, Cliff discovered a broken bolt on the engine mount which would have caused a vibration and changed the sound of the engine. After the work was completed on the major's plane, Cliff left a Post Mechanics Check Flight or PMCF with Major Poole's office at HQ.

Leaving HQ, Cliff saw Agnes walking by the lake. "Hey Aggie, how's your day going?"

"Oh, Cliff, I was just taking a walk before the next meal prep. I just needed some quiet time. What have you been doing at HQ, getting into trouble and being sent to the principal's office?"

"Very funny, Aggie! No, as a matter of fact, I found a serious problem with the major's plane. I just left the paperwork with Major Poole's office."

"Hey, I think that makes you a hero!"

Cliff shook his head and smiled sadly at Agnes, "No, the heroes are the guys fighting in the hedgerows of France and the Pacific islands – Corregidor, Midway, New Guinea, Guadalcanal, but I'm glad the major asks for me to take care of his plane. He's a fantastic pilot and just a great guy too." Cliff had gotten to know many of the pilots who flew into the base at High Wycombe. By and large, they were all brave guys who were just doing their jobs and didn't want any of the glory.

"Speaking of great guys, aren't you fixing dinner for General Eisenhower and Field Marshal Montgomery tomorrow night?" Cliff inquired, glad that the attention was no longer on him and what he had done today.

Agnes smiled and thought of all the responsibility that this dinner held for her and the girls, "Yes, as a matter of fact, the girls and I are preparing for the big dinner. It's such an honor and responsibility to make sure everything goes well."

Wanting to reassure Aggie that she was a fine cook and a heck of a wonderful woman, Cliff replied, "Hey, you'll do fine. You're one of the best cooks I know."

"You are just used to eating my fine cooking, so your opinion is a bit prejudiced, I think," Agnes laughed easily. "I do appreciate your compliments though," Agnes smiled at Cliff happily.

Cliff couldn't forget about all the damaged planes that had been coming into the airfield this week. "Hey, some of the guys were talking about the damage to the airplane factories in Stuttgart, Germany. Maybe that will slow down the Luftwaffe and help our pilots."

Agnes thought about Vera and how Stuttgart, Arkansas was so different from the Stuttgart she was just talking to Cliff about in Germany: Two names that were the same, Two very different places. I hope Vera is happy in her new camp; I haven't had a letter from her recently. Agnes was fortunate to have been sent here near Cliff. Breaking away from her thoughts, she noticed Cliff scanning the skies above them. I wonder what's wrong now.

Cliff looked up and took a quick glance at the plane circling the field above the base. Planes would sometimes circle the base if they couldn't land on the runway because of a problem with the plane. This plane didn't sound right. Cliff knew a lot about aircraft, and he thought he should get back to the hangar and see what the guys knew about this plane.

"Aggie, I need to get back to work now. See you later." Cliff smiled at Agnes and started backing away toward the hangar and the field adjacent to the hangar. Cliff looked concerned and worried.

Agnes thought, I wonder what's up with that plane. Cliff doesn't usually leave so suddenly. "Sure, Cliff, I'll see you later. Take care of yourself."

Cliff hurried and watched the plane overhead. There were several different problems that could occur with bombers. The bomb bay doors could be stuck with a live bomb in the rack. In that case, pilots would be instructed to try to land in the field. They would keep the plane away from the buildings and the staff near the landing strip. These were dangerous situations for both aircraft crews and people on the ground.

As Cliff approached the hangar, he saw other mechanics also looking up at the wounded plane. He always hated these situations. They were tricky to resolve so that everyone had a good outcome.

"Hey, John, what's happening with that plane? Obviously, it doesn't sound right, and they are asking the pilot to circle the field. Are they trying to burn extra fuel in preparation for an emergency landing?"

"Yes, Cliff, they don't want it to try to land with a load of fuel. It has a bomb stuck in the rack, and they can't get the landing gear to come down correctly."

The guys watched the plane helplessly as finally it came in for a belly landing in the adjacent field. The guys held their breath as the fire truck headed out to the plane hoping that they wouldn't be needed or that the plane wouldn't blow up. Finally, the plane was safely on the ground, and the crews were running toward the hangar. This incident would have a happy ending. Cliff headed over to talk to the lucky pilot. It would be a good day after all. Unfortunately, many Allied pilots were lost because of enemy fire.

Eisenhower Dinner

High Wycombe, England

May 1943

General Dwight D. Eisenhower was Supreme Allied Commander of the Allied Expeditionary Forces and in charge of the June 6, 1944 landings during the D-Day invasion in France.

Chapter 5

"Midge, Emily, and Ruth, we need to start saving some steaks for the dinner for General Eisenhower, the British delegation, and his various aides. I have ordered some special items from the commissary. They will be delivered on Tuesday. I know he isn't just any general; however, he wants to be treated like all the other GIs. The truth is he isn't like all the other servicemen – he is the Commander-in-chief of the Allied Expeditionary Forces in England," said Agnes.

Ruth replied, "I think that warrants more than a bologna sandwich! So, what's on the menu, Agnes?"

"Well, as I mentioned before, sirloin steak, mashed potatoes, green beans, Emily's homemade rolls, and a special chocolate cake for dessert. What do you think, Ruth?"

"Will there be any important British top brass coming for dinner as well? Maybe, Field Marshall Montgomery for instance. I think there's an important mission coming up. That's usually why there are so many meetings and security is tightened," Ruth indicated importantly.

1800 hours ~

The distinguished table of top brass were all seated and ready for the dinner the girls had spent time preparing in addition to their usual cooking duties. The normal dinner hour had been moved back an hour to allow the Eisenhower dinner to be undisturbed and was guarded by two sentries at each door.

Agnes remarked, "I think we have all the food prepared correctly, and it's all served to the men. I will make sure the cake is cut and put on plates. You girls can serve it as soon as they are finished with their meal." Going to the cabinet to take down the plates they reserved for special occasions, Agnes cut large slices of the gooey rich chocolate cake made from her grandmother's recipe her mother had sent in her last letter.

"Oh, by the way, Ruth, bring that platter of cloverleaf rolls. The basket is empty again. I think they like your homemade rolls for sure!" Agnes laughed easily.

Ruth grabbed the warm buttery rolls and headed for the table of officers, "Here are some more cloverleaf rolls. How about some fresh hot coffee?"

After all the dinner dishes were cleared, Midge passed out the thick slices of chocolate cake and more hot coffee to the officers. "Does anyone need anything else?" Ruth asked.

"Yes, send out the Mess Sergeant in charge of the dinner," General Eisenhower's Aide remarked to Ruth solemnly.

Ruth replied quietly, "Yes, sir. Right away!"

Coming through the kitchen door, Ruth whispered quietly, "Agnes, General Eisenhower's Aide wants to see YOU. He didn't seem very happy, and I am so sorry if I did anything! I didn't spill anything on the General...I'm sure of that. Do you want me to come with you?" Giving Ruth her best reassuring smile, Agnes took a glance at her hair and inspected her clothes for food spills. It wouldn't do to be scolded with food on her clothes. She took off her apron and took a deep breath ready for whatever was to come.

"No, Ruth, I'm sure you didn't do anything. Whatever he wants I will take care of it. Maybe the food didn't please him...the steaks were the best we could get around here. Okay, I will go face the firing squad. You tell Cliff if I'm put in the brig."

Agnes smiled at Ruth, squared her shoulders and walked out to meet General Eisenhower's Aide. She was confident that the food had been prepared to the best of their ability, but she would take the heat. Whatever she had to do she would keep her job as Mess Sergeant. What could the generals and advisors be upset about, Agnes thought on the long walk out to see them.

As she reached the table cluttered with empty cake plates and napkins, Agnes replied solemnly, "I am Corporal Taylor, and in charge of the kitchen. How can I help you, sir?"

"Corporal Taylor, I just wanted to tell you this is the best meal we have had in a year, probably longer than that, but don't tell my wife, I said that! Great job, Corporal. Good food is such a morale booster for the troops and the officers now. General Eisenhower just wanted me to personally commend you on a job well done."

Trying to remain professional although she privately was thrilled with the Aide's compliments, "I will let the rest of my staff know how pleased the men were with the food. Thank you, sir." Turning to leave, she couldn't keep the smile from completing her pink complexion.

Returning to the kitchen, "Girls, we just received the best compliment from General Eisenhower's staff. They loved the meal! Midge, thanks for keeping Frankie occupied and out of sight. It might have been a disaster if Frankie had gotten loose and crashed the dinner party tonight!" Agnes looked over at the sleeping Frankie and thought about how cute he looked.

"Well, I gave him a steak bone to chew on while the generals were eating. That kept him out of the way for a while. An out of control German dog would be difficult to explain – no matter how good the meal was tonight." Midge laughed.

"Okay, girls, let's get this mess cleaned up and get ready for tomorrow's breakfast. How do freshly baked cinnamon rolls, bacon, and cereal sound for tomorrow? Emily can get started on the yeast dough now and let it rise," Agnes stated.

"Sounds great to me," Emily replied, happy the pressure was off the girls. "I'll get started putting the rolls together first thing in the morning." She loved serving the warm cinnamon rolls to the men and women who appreciated the delicious treats so much. Not many people knew she was a such a softie. Lieutenant MacGregor just thought she was a discipline problem.

"Emily, are you okay or just tired? You look so sad right now. Is there anything you would like to share?"

"Well, Aggie, before we left New York, I received a letter from my mom about a soldier friend who was missing or killed. She didn't have a lot of information, and I still don't know what has happened. Thanks for listening and noticing I wasn't myself. My mother's last letter stated they still hadn't heard any more information."

"Sure, we all need someone to talk to occasionally." She gave Emily a hug and a smile.

"Okay, now to the pots and pans from this dinner tonight." Agnes announced as she headed to the large steel sink and began to scrub on the dirty pots and pans.

Agnes thought to herself: *my family will never believe I got to cook for one of the most famous generals in the Army. His compliment was worth all the work and time spent on that meal. This was better than a medal!*

Midge came over to tell Agnes goodbye, "Agnes, brilliant job today on the bloody good meal. I guess American cooking is okay after all."

"Thanks, Midge. Rest well. We have another busy day tomorrow!"

"Jeepers! I think it has been a long time since they have had some decent food. I thought you were a goner for sure when he called you out to his table. That was nice of the fellas to be so complimentary to us," said Ruth.

The Birthday Party

May 17, 1943

Military life can evoke feelings of homesickness and loneliness for many soldiers based in foreign countries. Items associated with home: birthday parties, presents, letters, and friendly greetings help to decrease battle fatigue.

Chapter 6

Cliff came into the Mess Hall for his morning break; he thought, I don't see any coffee on the side table. Suddenly, several pilots, navigators, and mechanics jumped out of the kitchen followed by Agnes, Emily, Midge, and Ruth. Agnes was carrying a huge chocolate birthday cake.

"Everyone, sing Happy Birthday to Cliff!"

After the singing had ended, Cliff said, "Aggie, this was the most exciting birthday I have ever had! You know there was never money for birthday parties at my house. This is just wonderful. You are the best girl around here...or anywhere else! I'm so glad you are here."

"Well, everyone likes a party! Let all the guys at the hangars know there is birthday cake over here. I'm sure they will want to celebrate with you when they have a break today," Agnes smiled at Cliff.

Walking back into the kitchen, Agnes thought, I guess we need to get this place cleaned up for the dinner meal coming up soon. I'll ask if anyone wants more coffee or cake before I put it on the side table for the next group of hungry aviators. Agnes started to put forks and plates on the side table as people began to get back to work.

As she busied herself with cleaning the kitchen, Emily came into the kitchen, "Hey, Agnes, go talk to Cliff while Ruth and I get started on the dishes. You two don't get to spend much time together."

Agnes smiled and said, "Thanks, Emily!" Agnes took Emily's offer and went out to find Cliff. Spotting him sitting alone finishing up his last bite of chocolate cake, she went over to Cliff, "You know, I still have your graduation picture in my pocket. I have never forgotten what a great day that was for your family. Your mom was so proud of you. I'm afraid that it has gotten bent a little on the corners."

Looking at the small wrinkled photo, Cliff said, "Why do you still have my graduation picture with you, Aggie?"

Agnes thought, oh no! How could she have been so stupid. Now, Cliff is going to know I have a crush on him. I should never have brought the graduation picture of Cliff. How will I explain this now?

"Ehh...well, I thought I might not recognize you after not seeing you for a while. You know people change...." Agnes had to think quickly. She didn't want Cliff to know how much she had missed him. "Today, I have it with me because I thought the guys might want to see what you looked like in 1937 when you graduated." Agnes, at a loss for words, was glad that Cliff didn't notice how red her face had suddenly become. She was never very good when she was put on the spot.

Thankfully, Midge and Ruth came over to look at Cliff's graduation picture. "Hey, Cliff you changed one uniform for another didn't you? Quite nice!" said Midge. Now Agnes could move on to check how the refreshments were holding out and if anything needed to be added to the table.

The guys were looking at the graduation picture and joking with Cliff when she heard, "Oh yes, you probably don't know that Aggie was the Salutatorian of our senior class at Hermitage Springs School. She's a very smart girl, but I'm sure you all knew that by now!"

Overhearing Cliff brag about Agnes was sure a surprise. I wonder why he remembered our high school days now. She certainly had to set the record straight...

"Oh, Cliff...come on! There were only twelve people in our class that year. It was a very small school, Midge and Ruth. Cliff named the yearbook the *Skyline*, and it still has that name now. I think he was thinking ahead to someday being around airplanes!" Agnes remarked jokingly.

"Gee, all this talk of home has stirred up a lot of memories for me. I have a great mom and family. I miss them but don't have the money to go back for a visit. It's been almost two years since I have seen them," Cliff said sadly.

Seeing Cliff's face drop, she said, "Hey, I'm sorry to make you sad on your twenty-sixth birthday!"

"That's okay, Aggie. You couldn't be mean if you tried. You're the nicest person I know. Look, you just threw a birthday party for me! No one has ever done that before! Well, unfortunately, I must go back to work. Can I see you after work, Aggie?"

"Sure. I'll make sure I get my menus done..."

Ruth and Emily looked at each other in a conspiratorial way as each thought, *we will make sure she makes it.* Cliff and Agnes deserved to be together and anyone who looked at them could tell they cared for each other a great deal.

The Mess Hall door opened again, and Mac came in smiling, "Hey, am I too late to join the party? I want to wish one of the best mechanics around a happy birthday!"

Giving Mac a greeting and a smile, Aggie replied, "Not too late. I'll get you a piece of chocolate cake right away," Agnes went to the table and cut a large piece of cake and grabbed a cup of coffee for the late arrival.

Hey, Mac, come meet a good friend of mine, Agnes Taylor."

"Agnes, this is Mac another ace plane mechanic from Terre Haute, Indiana. Whenever we need something way up high, we call on Mac to retrieve it for us. Mac is six foot six inches tall. He really wanted to be a pilot but was too tall, so he did the next best thing – become an airplane mechanic."

"Hiya, Agnes, very glad to meet you. Looking at Cliff, I would say you two are very good friends, and I'm pretty sure I'll see you around a lot."

"I'm sure you will, too, because I'm a cook here at the Mess Hall. So, unless you're dieting or fasting, you'll see a lot of me around the base," remarked Agnes smiling at Mac and handing him the cake.

"Oh, thanks Agnes. That birthday cake looks great," Mac replied eyeing the thick slice of cake. Chocolate cake was one of his favorite desserts. He hadn't had many opportunities to eat chocolate cake in the Army.

Mac and Cliff sat down to talk as Mac ate a big bite of cake. "Cliff, we only have a few days left to get our hours in to get flight pay this month. I am going up this afternoon if I can schedule a ride. That extra ten dollars a month will sure help my family. I'll send it to my wife Ruth. How about you?"

"No. Good luck to you though. Say, Mac, I need to get back to the hangar right now. See you later, pal." Rising to leave, Cliff looked for Agnes and spotting her cleaning tables; he gave her a wave and left Mac finishing his piece of cake.

Agnes walked over to Emily and said happily, "I guess this birthday party was a success!"

Agnes started cleaning up the leftover dishes and putting silverware in the trays. It had been a fabulous idea to surprise Cliff because he deserved all the praise he got. The days ahead may become crazy busy, and it was good he could relax and enjoy some cake and fellowship with the guys. The guys didn't get a lot of opportunities to enjoy special treats these days. How much longer is this war going to continue?

Lunch at the Mess Hall ~

Edie Slate silently contemplated what she had read this morning in the memo. Her job was vitally important to the war effort and extremely urgent she keep her duties to herself. It had been boring and lonely with just two other girls to talk to every day. She couldn't even tell her family what work she did over here.

"Would you like a refill on your coffee?" came a soft sweet Southern voice like hers. There were lots of British accents, but not many Southern girls at High Wycombe.

"Oh, sure, that would be great. Thanks," Edie replied softly to the young woman about her age holding a coffee pot in her hand. Edie had started her war department job soon after graduation and was eager to see the world; however, the world she saw was very limited to one or two rooms and no contact with many other people.

Agnes topped off the girl's cup of coffee and lingered just a few seconds as she debated whether to say more. This gal sure looked sad. Should she intrude on her thoughts or move on? As the girl looked up at her with troubled brown eyes, Edie said, "How long have you been here?"

That's the opening Aggie was looking for, so she sat down opposite the woman and said, "I've been here since March '43, and it takes some getting used to. The guys are friendly and grateful for the warm meals we put out. That doesn't happen everywhere."

Agnes was reluctant to pry but felt perhaps this new arrival needed to talk to someone... "What's your name?" Agnes smiled at the pretty young woman sympathetically.

"Edie Slate," she replied simply. "I'm from Summer Shade, Kentucky; originally I spent some time in Washington D.C. doing some...hmm, training before I was assigned to work here."

Thinking they had a lot in common as Southern women, she hoped they could be friends too. This woman looked like she could use a good friend. It was hard to be so far away from family - she knew that for sure. Most military or civilians didn't have the money to go home on leave.

Edie got up to leave as she finished her last sip of coffee, Agnes touched Edie's arm gently and said, "Hey, if you ever want to talk, my name's Aggie. You know where to find me," she laughed slightly and smiled warmly.

Edie's eyes filled with tears as she said, "Thanks," and rushed to leave the Mess Hall.

Agnes looked after the quiet young woman wondering why Edie was always so quiet. She had seen Edie eating alone in the Mess Hall before but felt awkward talking to her. She was glad she had made the effort to be a friend today. Maybe she would open up more the next time the opportunity arose. War was a difficult time for everyone.

~~~~~~~~

Rushing out of the Mess Hall before she embarrassed herself by breaking down in tears, Edie dried her eyes and walked down to the lake. It was a serene place which settled her nerves. The burden of never discussing her work was weighing on her mind. The other two girls were kind, but never talked about anything. They wrote letters to their families or read books in their free time. The loneliness was like an anchor threatening to drop her to the bottom of the sea surrounding this island of Britain. Aggie's comforting words were tempting, but...she couldn't explain her work to anyone. Getting to know Aggie was a bright spot in her day. She looked forward to spending more time in her company.

After decoding a disturbing German message yesterday, Edie couldn't sleep. She kept recounting the details of the bombing over and over. Civilians were sometimes sacrificed when important sites were bombed. The Norden Bombsight was an important development to improve accuracy. Unfortunately, hitting the target one hundred percent of the time wasn't possible.

Edie found herself walking slowly back to the Campbell House where she and the other two women were billeted away from the other females. The Air Force Engineer was assigned to this building, but there was room for the code girls to work upstairs unnoticed for the most part. They also lived in the close quarters across the hall from where they spend hours poring over secret papers. It was imperative that others not guess what their mission was here at the base. Their work was important and had to be protected at all costs.

Coming to England was by far the farthest she had even been away from home, unless the trip to Indianapolis to visit relatives counts. Indianapolis had seemed like a large city compared to her hometown. Her cousin had shown her around the city with Monument Circle and the L.S. Ayres department store being a couple highlights. Her cousin was a cadette at the USO (United Service Organization) Union Station Canteen. Her cousin Grace enjoyed dancing with the soldiers who came to the canteen for a reprieve from the war.

Maybe she would write Grace and her parents a letter tonight. Her parents lived on a farm and missed her help with the chores. She had helped her mother, Emma, finish a Dresden Plate quilt before she left home. It was her favorite design. She sure wished she had one of those warm and comfy quilts wrapped around her now.

Frankie's Finale

July 1, 1943

"On July 1, 1943, WAAC, Women's Army Auxiliary Corps, was given active duty status, becoming WAC. Nearly 150,000 American women served in the Women's Army Corps during World War II."

Chapter 7

Once the Germans started bombing London and the surrounding areas, many families began sending their children to the countryside for protection from the danger of bombs. Thus, it was often referred to as 'Operation Pied Piper' after the folktale written by the Brothers Grimm. Many British civilians were killed from these raids. It was reported that in 1942 nearly two thousand civilians were injured by enemy action. Farm families and other citizens cared for these children, often for several years, until it was deemed safe for them to return to their families.

The next day~

I guess I'll head over to the Mess Hall and get things started before the rest of the girls get there. I'd like to spend some time with Frankie too.

Entering the Mess Hall, Agnes headed to the kitchen to find out what Frankie had been up to during the night. As she entered the kitchen, she found him sleeping peacefully, curled up on the towels under the prep table. "Hi Little Guy, did you have a good sleep?" Frankie answered by jumping up and licking Agnes' face. Laughing, Agnes took him outside for a while to take care of his business and get some exercise.

"Are you hungry, Frankie? How about some leftovers while I get breakfast started for everyone?" Reaching down to pick the little dog up and give him a gentle hug, she heard the kitchen door open suddenly.

"Aggie, who are you talking to? Is that a dog? What the ...?" Cliff stopped abruptly and stared at the wriggly little dog in Agnes' arms.

"Hi Cliff. This is Frankie, and he's our little mascot of the kitchen. Isn't he just the cutest thing you have ever seen?"

"Yes, he is cute. I'll agree to that, but Aggie do you know what would happen if Lieutenant MacGregor saw him or found out you were feeding him food from the mess? You must get rid of him. You could lose your stripes or worse if the higher ups wanted to make an example of you – since you oversee the Mess Hall. Didn't you read your regulations? He's a health hazard!" Cliff said loudly.

"No, he is not a health hazard! We gave him a bath, and he doesn't touch the food or anything like that," her voice raising in volume to match Cliff's as she explained things to him. They hadn't argued or disagreed often, but he didn't have to be so brusque about this situation with the dog.

"Okay, you take the risk if you want, but if you have any common sense you will get rid of him today. That's just my opinion, of course. I have to go before I say something, I will regret...I'll see you later today," Cliff remarked tersely and marched out of the kitchen.

Agnes picked up Frankie and rubbed his wiry hair letting a tear roll down her cheek. "Frankie, what am I going to do with you?" She sat him down and prepared a dish of sausages for him to eat while she thought about what to do next.

After Frankie finished eating, Agnes picked up his bowl and said to him, "Okay, Frankie, where can I take you, so you will be loved and wanted?" Agnes said sadly. Frankie looked up at Agnes with big sad eyes and licked Agnes' fingers sensing that she was upset.

When Emily, Midge, and Ruth arrived, Agnes told them what Cliff had said this morning. Reluctantly, they all agreed that something had to be done today. "There's someone knocking on the back door, Midge. Do you want to see who's there?" Agnes asked.

"Come in, please. Those vegetables look quite nice, Mrs. Clarke! We haven't had any fresh vegetables for a week," Midge added. "Agnes, Mrs. Clarke is here with our local produce that you ordered. Look at the beautiful carrots and those luscious red tomatoes."

"Good morning, Mrs. Clarke. Thanks for bringing my order today. The vegetables look wonderful! I'll have the girls bring in the rest of the order while I have you sign the purchase order. Have a seat while I get it from my desk."

Mrs. Clarke was a stout woman with the complexion of someone who had worked outside much of her life. Her skin was red, and small thin lines had started to form around her eyes. On her previous visit she mentioned that she was housing some of the children who were evacuees from London at her farm. "What a sweet little dog you have here. Is it okay if I pet him? I just love dachshunds! I haven't had a dog since my little Westie died a couple years ago. Come here, little guy, let me love on you a bit," Mrs. Clarke crooned to the wiggly little dog as she pulled him up to her ample chest.

Agnes looked at the charming picture of homeless dog and lonely woman. An idea started to form in her mind. It looks like this woman could use someone to love too. I wonder if she would be willing to help us out. "Mrs. Clarke, I have to find a permanent home for Frankie today. Would you like to take Frankie with you? It would sure help me out," Agnes pleaded.

"Oh, my dear, I don't know if I should do that." Mrs. Clarke looked at the cute dog adoringly and rubbed his ears. She seemed to be thinking over the idea of a new pet. Cubby, a little girl staying at her farm, would love to have a lively dog like that to help her forget all the misery she had seen during the bombing. It's a lot for a small child to deal with, she mused.

She wondered if this could be the medicine Cubby needs to help her forget about the war for a while. It's really all she's known. A dog wouldn't replace a mum, but it sure would give her something to love. She should do it, she thought.

Sometimes families became separated or there was no home to return to in London. It was indeed sad for the children to be uprooted and apart from their parents. At times, parents felt like they missed a large part of their child's childhood. When they return to their families after the war, there will be an adjustment for their families who were almost like strangers to the children.

"He is darling, though isn't he? Hmmm. Okay, I can do that, if you are sure you want me to take him." Mrs. Clarke was hoping she was doing the right thing. Another mouth to feed was something to consider, but things always seemed to work out. She was glad she could help by taking the little dachshund from these stressed ladies.

Agnes gave a huge sigh of relief as this was an answer to her problem, "It would sure be a blessing if I knew he was going to a good home. It would be easier for all the girls in the kitchen," Agnes explained to the kind British woman sitting in her kitchen.

Ruth, Midge, and Emily brought in the vegetables and Agnes explained that Mrs. Clarke was taking Frankie home with her. Ruth couldn't believe that Mrs. Clarke was willing to help them with Frankie. "That's a brilliant idea!" The very British Midge declared to the group of women gathered in the kitchen.

Mrs. Clarke signed the purchase order for the vegetables and picked up Frankie. "Goodbye, Frankie. Be a good boy for Mrs. Clarke." Agnes wiped her eyes and turned away quickly. The other girls also gave Frankie a goodbye hug. Without lingering any longer, Mrs. Clarke scooped up Frankie and put him in her large wicker vegetable basket and hurried out of the kitchen.

Cubby was a very smart child but being away from her parents for two years was very difficult for her. She missed her mum and two older brothers; however, she remembered coming home from school and wondering if her house would still be there. Mrs. Clarke was very kind; unfortunately, she didn't make the same food as Cubby was used to eating. Living in the country was very different from the busy bustling city of London. Her family hadn't been able to come see her for a while with the petrol rationing; trips to the country being very limited.

Mrs. Clarke hurried back to her wagon of vegetables with a smile on her face as she placed the wicker basket of squirming fur on the wagon seat. She was eager to show the wriggly little dog to eleven-year old Cubby. Suddenly, the lid sprung open, a small wiggly dachshund appeared and licked Cubby's face. "Oh, aren't you a pretty little thing," she said laughing at his entertaining antics.

"Do you like him, my dear?"

"Oh yes! He's so sweet. Can we keep him?" Cubby looked at the wiry little dog and thought of her dog, Zelda, at home in London. She missed her almost as much as her parents. Zelda was small and wiry like this wee dog too. Maybe living in the country was not going to be so bad after all. Cubby was fortunate to live with a family she already knew.

Maggie was the other child the Clarke family had brought into their home. Mrs. Clarke's family was kind to Maggie and her. Maggie's mum was able to visit often and stayed with the Clarkes for a few weeks also.

"Oh, positively we can. He was part of the trade today," Mrs. Clarke replied as she nestled him among her wares. She thought, Frankie is a fine name for this animal. Maybe she could coax a tiny smile from the thin lips of a little homesick British girl she had taken into her home and her heart.

Ten-year old Maggie who was small for her age and preferred to be by herself. Maggie had elected to stay on the farm today to take care of the ponies. One of the girls' favorite activities was riding the ponies around the farm. I think she will be delighted to see Frankie too. Maggie was a very shy young girl. Perhaps, having a lively dog to add to the animals on the farm will be a wonderful present for everyone.

"Oh Mrs. Clarke, would it be okay if I held Frankie on my lap?" Cubby asked hopefully.

"Well, sure it would, wee girl," Mrs. Clarke had been quite daft not to have thought of it first. Children and dogs have a way of fitting together like salt and pepper. Hmm, I wonder if Mr. Clarke will think that I have made a brilliant decision or not. I will have to convince him that I didn't have any other choice. I'll have to cook a splendid dinner for him tonight. Perhaps she could prepare a special treat, Summer Pudding. Her husband dearly loved the sweet dessert.

British summer pudding consists of white bread lined in a bowl and covered with fruit and fruit juice. It is soaked overnight, and then the bowl is turned onto a plate. It is a very tasty summer dessert.

Frankie, a very friendly dog, seemed to be very adaptable to wherever he was being sent. Mrs. Clarke hoped that her quick decision to take the dog wouldn't stretch her already thin budget. Well, she would make it work for the sake of these little girls. They had been through enough since the war started. This seemed to be the best medicine for what was ailing them today.

At least little Cubby's face was happy as she held the cuddly dog on her lap gently rubbing his head. It had been a wonderful day for them both. Promises were sometimes broken, and so were small hearts.

Later in the day~

Entering the Mess Hall, Cliff came up to Agnes and asked if he could talk to her alone. Moving off to a vacant area of the room, "Aggie, I'm sorry I was so harsh this morning. I was only thinking of you and your career. Please forgive me," Cliff said regretfully.

As much as she wanted to hang on to her disappointment and sadness, she knew letting Frankie go was the right thing to do. "Sure, Cliff. I know it was the correct thing to do. I just wanted to keep him because he needed a home, and we wanted to love on him.

You understand, don't you? I never could stay mad at you."

Cliff gave Agnes a crooked smile and look of concern. "Of course, I understand; he was a cute little dog. What did you do with him?"

Thinking quickly and hoping to get back at Cliff just a little bit for his earlier comments, Agnes responded promptly, "We turned him over to the Germans." Cliff looked shocked as Agnes grinned at his exasperated face.

"Okay, I deserved that, but let's have a truce about Frankie."

Agnes agreed to the terms of the truce and explained Mrs. Clarke stopped by this morning to deliver some vegetables, and she loved Frankie. She told Cliff the British lady was caring for two young evacuee girls from London who needed a frisky dog more than we did. Agnes explained she agreed to take him for us. Agnes went on to say, "It was sad; I have to tell you...but it was for the best I know."

"Aggie let's take a walk after you are off duty. I'll stop by the Mess Hall and pick you up around 1900. Okay?"

"That should be fine, Cliff. I have something to tell you." Agnes smiled as she walked back into the Mess Hall clearing dishes and starting to clean up after dinner.

"Emily, I need to leave at 1900 hours. With all the excitement of the Eisenhower dinner, I forgot about the Escape Kit we found in our gear. I want to talk to Cliff about it and find out who left it with us," whispered Agnes.

"Did you hide it well? I don't want anyone to find it until we discover who it belongs to, and why they didn't turn it in during debriefing. Don't military personnel have to turn those kits in to their superiors?"

Agnes explained what she knew about Escape Kits to Emily. She said they were given to pilots or soldiers who could be captured. They contained items that could be used to help someone in a dangerous situation. Kits, just like the one we have, usually have a passport size picture and some gold. It's all sealed in rubber. "Who could it belong to?" asked Agnes mysteriously.

"But...the kit has the picture missing. Clearly, someone doesn't want to be identified," stated Emily. "I wonder if it's someone that we know. Maybe someone who has eaten here in our mess. Check with Cliff and get his ideas on this mystery. Do you think we should tell Lieutenant MacGregor?"

Agnes gave that idea some thought and replied, "I think it is best to talk to Cliff about the Escape Kit, then see what he thinks about all this."

Emily, with the wild imagination, said, "I wonder if the Escape Kit belongs to a mysterious spy or a handsome double agent working for Germany."

"Oh, Emily! You are impossible sometimes!" said Agnes.

A Coded Message

October 1943

"The Air Transport Auxiliary (ATA) female pilots – the women who flew Spitfires and many other types of planes from factories to RAF squadrons during World War II."

Chapter 8

Ella Cook had always loved flying and was delighted to come to England to see the Wings for Britain program. Lieutenant MacGregor oversaw the women on base, and she needed to speak with her immediately.

"Come in and sit down, Miss Cook," Lieutenant MacGregor said.

"Thank you for seeing me so quickly. I have a problem I am hoping you can help me with. I'll just get to the point. I found a note on the airplane when I was making my exit check. I need someone to decode it and follow up with whatever it says.   I don't want to go to the general as he has enough to think about now, and I don't think it's so serious he should be bothered. Do you have a someone who can do this job?"

"I see, Miss Cook. There is one WAC who is responsible and gets the job done. In fact, she was able to please General Eisenhower with a wonderful meal he is still talking about. Her name is Corporal Agnes Taylor and in charge of the mess on base. You may want to introduce yourself and tell her about the note."

"Thanks, lieutenant. I will go over there now. because I could use something to eat too."

"Good luck to you, Miss Cook."

At the Mess Hall ~

"Aggie, I think we are going to have some important visitors again today," Ruth stated.

"Why, do you think that?"

"I just saw a B-24 land over at the field," said Ruth wearily. "You can tell by the sound of their engines."

As Midge walked into the room, Agnes filled her in on what the girls had been discussing. "Perhaps, we'll be feeding some big brass again today." Agnes thought to herself that maybe some important military campaign had been planned right here in her Mess Hall.

"I always knew food was the key to everything that ails a man," laughed blonde-haired Ruth.

Emily and Midge came in laughing about something Frankie had done the day before. "Hi, everyone, I'm on the way to the stove to fry bacon: I'm still tired from cleaning up the kitchen yesterday," Emily remarked.

A few hours later...

Agnes thought about what one of the WACs had told her about women in the Russian army. They sure have it tougher than we do. The Russian women were assigned to jobs as fighter pilots, tank drivers, infantry, and anti-aircraft gunners. The Russian people were starving, and at least the women would get to eat if they joined the military. Many of the Russian male soldiers had been killed or captured so it was important for the women to help in the war effort. We are lucky to be safe in Britain. The slamming door interrupted her thoughts as she heard some female voices call out.

"Hey, can a couple American gals get a bite to eat around here?" shouted two exhausted looking women pilots walking in the door of the Mess Hall and dropping their gear near a clean table.

Watching the two women head their way, "Sure," replied Agnes. "Hi, I'm Corporal Agnes Taylor, head of the kitchen, and this is Ruth King and Midge Whitethorpe who are with the RAF. Emily Smith is also part of the crew. We keep the fellas fed around here." Agnes, with red hair swinging, nodded toward Ruth, Midge and Emily.

"Glad to meet all of you ladies. I'm Ella Cook, and this is my co-pilot, Lois Lovelace."

"Glad to meet you, too. Always good to have some more gals around here," said Ruth happily.

"Are you some of the women pilots who arrived with Jacqueline Cochran? Are you involved with the WASPs? What brings you and Lois to England?" exclaimed Agnes.

"Whoa, girls! Let me get my feet on the ground before you pummel me with so many questions! Yes, Lois and I are here with a dozen other American women to see how the Brits run their women's training program. So, we have had a long journey from America."

The British program, *Wings for Britain*, had been going on in England for a while. The girls came over to see what they could learn. They wanted to get a similar program started in the United States. As one can imagine, there were some pilots and other men who were not excited about women and aircraft. The women knew they could be of help with aviation and the war effort if they could just be given a chance.

"So, we'll see what happens after our visit here," replied Ella wearily.

"Well, that sounds fantastic! I hope it works out for you and the other women aviators. Midge knows a lot about the RAF women here in England. You may want to talk to her as well," Agnes replied.

Since December 1941, British women had been conscripted, or required to do war work, when the British Parliament passed the National Service Act, requiring unmarried women ages 20-30 to join the armed forces, work in a factory or work on the land with the Women's Land Army. British women did some of the same jobs as American women – cooks, drivers, postal workers, and radar operators.

Agnes, always wanting to make people comfortable and fed, asked the newcomers, "Are you gals hungry?

We have some pork chops and potatoes left from lunch. How does that sound to you two?"

"Sure! That would be swell because it's been a long time since we had breakfast," said Ella and Lois hungrily.

"Coming right up!" said Ruth graciously. "Have a seat anywhere. The ladies' facilities are out back if you need to clean up after your long flight."

Lois thought a trip to freshen up after their long flight sounded perfect. "Thanks, Ruth, I think I will. I could use a few minutes to put myself back together," laughed Lois. "Are you coming, Ella?"

"You go ahead, Lois. I might be there later."

Ella was hoping for some time alone with Agnes, so she could talk to her about a situation which had arisen shortly after she and Lois landed.

After Lois left for the ladies' room, Ella said to Agnes, "You seem like a trustworthy person. Have you heard any scuttlebutt about something big going on here at High Wycombe?" Agnes took a few seconds to give her answer some thought. She wasn't a gossiping woman, and she wanted to get to know Ella a little more before she confided any information she may have heard.

Agnes started to say something when Cliff walked into the Mess Hall. "Where could I get a cup of cold, weak left-over coffee?" said soft-spoken Cliff with a chuckle.

Giving Cliff her prettiest smile, Agnes replied sarcastically, "Well, when you put it that way, we keep our best brew for the top brass. How are you doing, Cliff?"

"Everyone wants everything done yesterday. I had to take a break for a few minutes."

"Cliff, meet one of the American pilots, Ella Cook. She just flew in this afternoon for the *Wings for Britain* program. Good to have more females around here with all these demanding guys," joked Agnes. "Cliff is an airplane mechanic from my hometown of Red Boiling Springs, Tennessee. They keep him busy working on the planes, and he keeps them flying."

"We must not be that terrible if you volunteered to come all the way to England to fight this war," Cliff teased.

"Oh, some of you guys are okay."

"Just okay?" hooted Cliff. Cliff poured himself a cup of coffee and sat down for a few minutes to discuss the flight over from the United States with Ella.

Ella asked Cliff, "How are things going over here? We never get accurate information about the war. By the time it reaches us, it has changed or just not right."

"Well, the guys and I are kept really busy keeping the planes in the air. Some of the planes barely make it back here – they are so shot up and in need of help. We do what we can to patch them up. These pilots are the best. They are fearless!"

"Ella, how are things in the states?" Cliff asked. News of home was always welcome to service people overseas.

"We are doing all we can, I guess. We are thankful for all you do."

The U.S. government was selling war bonds and people were helping as much as they could afford. Rationing was hard on the civilians on the home front too, but no one was shooting at most American citizens in the states. The military was thankful our people were saving tin and tires to build more planes and tanks.

"Speaking of which, I should go back to work. We'll talk later," said Cliff happily. "Nice to meet you Ella and good luck to you and the other lady aviators."

Ella didn't have to wait long for Lois to appear again. Lois, slamming the door on her way back into the Mess Hall, said, "I could eat a horse! Is it about ready?" Agnes and Ella couldn't finish their conversation which would have to wait to later when they were alone.

About that time, Ruth returned carrying two trays of steaming food for Ella and Lois. "What about the other girls who came with you? I'm sure they are hungry too," questioned Ruth. "We have plenty in the kitchen whenever they want to come by."

Swallowing a mouthful of delicious pork chop, "Yes, they will probably be stopping in later after they get our gear stowed away," Ella replied.

"Well, girls, I'll leave you to eat while we get things started for supper and clean up from the lunch mess," said Agnes. "There's coffee over there, help yourself."

Ella and Lois dug into the creamy potatoes and pork chops. It had been quite a while since they had eaten. Twenty-five-year old Lois rubbed her honey blonde hair. "I'll be happy to get a hot shower and wash my dirty hair."

"I know," said Ella. "I feel like I'm covered in grime after today's trip."

Finishing up the last bite of her food Lois felt full and happy to get something to eat. She was hopeful she could get some rest soon. "Well, these chops are delicious. Hard to get decent chow in the military. These ladies know how to cook." Lois said grateful for the warm welcome from Agnes and her crew.

"Agree," Ella said chewing quietly. Agnes walked out to collect the empty trays and say goodbye to the girls. She reminded Ella to send the rest of the crew over to eat when she met up with them.

"Agnes, good to meet Ruth and you. I want to continue our conversation when you are off duty sometime soon," Ella said.

"My friends call me, Aggie. How long are you going to be here? I hope you find out what you need to know about the Wings for Britain program. The Brits are great people. We have some RAF pilots stationed here too."

"I'm not sure how long we will be here. I'll find you," said Ella and followed Lois out of the Mess Hall.

After finishing off their first real meal in twelve hours, the girls went to report to the commanding officer of the base and find the rest of their group. They had a lot to do and needed to make some arrangements for interviews.

~~~~~~~~

After Ella and Lois left, Ruth came out to sweep the floor. "Aggie, I don't know why the military won't let more women fly planes in non-combat areas."

"Well, we know we are smart enough," joked Agnes.

"Maybe that's what the guys are afraid of," replied Ruth. Ruth was from Dover and grew up with five brothers. She was used to dealing with men who tried to protect her.

"Why did you join up, Ruth?" said the tall red headed Agnes.

"I guess I'm just like the rest of the women here. I wanted to do my part to help in this war. This assignment is also a way for me to see some of the world. There wouldn't be a chance for me to go anywhere out of Dover. Say, Agnes, what's up with you and Cliff?" Ruth inquired. "Didn't you two know each other back home."

Thinking back to her life back home, Agnes reflected quickly about her answer, "Yes, in Tennessee. We used to date, but things just happen you know..." Agnes said sadly. "We went to the same high school and lived nearby each other. In our small town everyone knows each other. Cliff left high school to work in the CCC, you know, the Civilian Conservation Corps. That's the organization that builds public buildings and dams all over the United States. He came back and finished high school when I graduated. His folks were poor and after his dad died, his mother needed some money to keep things going. There are still seven more kids left at home. He sends most of his money home to his mom now. I think he felt he needed to care for his family, so he joined up."

"Maybe that flame can be ignited again?"

Of course, Agnes thought about getting back together with Cliff, but there were important things to do right now. Everyone had to be alert and watch each other's back. "Perhaps, we'll see, Ruth."

Agnes thought, I guess we better get back to work or there will be some hungry guys storming in here soon. After Ruth continued her sweeping, Agnes also started to wonder about what Ella wanted to tell her. Why was it so important to her?

That evening ~

After dinner Agnes decided to take a walk near the hangar. Cliff was just ending his shift and saw her walking determinedly outside his hangar.

"Hey, wait up, Red," shouted Cliff. "Does a fella have to race to catch up with you? I've been wanting to talk to you all day. I came over to get a cup of coffee, but you had a crowd."

Agnes updated Cliff on Ella and the other girls. "They seem to be great women pilots, and very brave to fly so far from home." Agnes thought how exciting it would be to fly one of those large planes all the way across the ocean.

"Yes, I heard about them from the other guys this afternoon. Some of the guys, of course not me, thought they were nice looking! We don't see many women here on the base. Did Ella Cook tell you why they are here?"

"Of course, you weren't looking at them, Cliff! You only have eyes for me...right?" Agnes laughed as Cliff turned red in the face. "Okay, I'll give you a break. Ella Cook told me that she and the other women flew over here to study what Britain was doing with their women pilots. She wants to get the women pilots involved in helping in the war effort. They aren't trying to take jobs that our men currently have...just want to be helpful to the United States in any way they can. They hope to take back some ideas that will fly with the Army Air Corps at home."

Looking at Agnes Cliff said, "Okay, that makes sense to me. Hey, Aggie, why did you come to England? There were easier places you could have requested," Cliff ventured easily.

Agnes thought over what Cliff said and selected her words carefully. She didn't want Cliff to think she was chasing after him. She always enjoyed his company and wanted them to be – at the very least – friends.

Agnes answered Cliff's question hesitatingly, "I don't know...I guess I wanted to see the world. You know, back when we were in high school, my favorite subjects were social studies and history. I want to know things, and there isn't a lot to see and know back in Tennessee. Besides after you left...."

Before Agnes could finish her sentence, a male voice boomed, "Hey, Cliff, you're wanted back in the hangar. There's a pilot who needs to talk with you," said William John McDonnel, more commonly known as Mac to his friends, walking over to where the couple were talking.

Cliff grimaced and replied to Mac, "Okay, I'll be right there. "Well, you have to go see a pilot about a plane, and I have to see some cooks about some food. See you both later."

"I guess I'll see you tomorrow. Take care of yourself." Cliff said, reluctant to leave Agnes and their warm conversation, as he gave a quick wave and jogged off to the hangar.

As Agnes walked back to the Mess Hall she thought, *I wonder why I didn't pick – the motor transport or a radio operator instead of a cook. I guess cooking for my sisters and brothers was good training for this job. Well, tomorrow it's up early to get breakfast started.*

The next day~

"Oh, Aggie, you just got a message delivered from Lieutenant MacGregor." Aggie picked up the message and read it quickly. She had a busy day ahead of her.

"Look, girls, I have to see Lieutenant MacGregor now. Cover for me, and I will be back as soon as I can." Picking up her hat, Aggie left the Mess Hall and hurried to Lieutenant MacGregor's office.

When she arrived, she was ushered into the lieutenant's office immediately. "Have a seat Corporal Taylor. Oh, I heard General Eisenhower was pleased with the meal. Good work."

"Thank you, Lieutenant MacGregor."

"You have a letter from headquarters. You may want to open it because it looks official...of course, everything the Army does is official."

Opening the letter carefully, Agnes said, "My promotion came through. Thank you, Lieutenant MacGregor. I'm sure you had something to do with this too."

"You earned it, Corporal Taylor. Well, I should address you as Sergeant Taylor now."

"Thank you, lieutenant."

"I have something else to discuss with you today." Agnes was getting nervous about why she was called here today. She wasn't used to all this attention.

Seeing Agnes' troubled face, the lieutenant said that she wasn't in trouble but was needed for a special mission. "I have a letter that I want you to carry to High Wycombe for me." Handing Agnes the sealed envelope, Lieutenant MacGregor said quickly. "It is a very important message to General Stevens. He is the commander in charge at Harlaxton Manor in Grantham, England, and he is waiting for this letter. You will be given a three-day pass and a jeep to take you there. You can select your own driver from the motor pool or someone else you trust to keep this confidential. Can I depend on you to keep this information to yourself, Taylor?"

"Absolutely, Lieutenant MacGregor," whispered Agnes quickly.

She left the lieutenant's office and started walking back to the Mess Hall, Agnes wondered, why she was selected from all the girls in the unit? It must be important if she was asked to perform this task. She would follow through with this assignment for Lieutenant MacGregor. It would give her a chance to see some of the British countryside on the way to Grantham too.

Of course, she would ask Cliff to accompany her to High Wycombe. It would be wonderful to spend more time with him, she thought.

On the way back to the Mess Hall, she thought, I must write a letter to my parents. They will be so proud of my promotion. They weren't excited to see me leave home. Great news!

Agnes returned in time for preparations for the evening meal at the Mess Hall. The girls were curious about Aggie's visit to Lieutenant MacGregor but were too polite to ask. Finally, Aggie said, "Girls, my promotion went through! I am now Sergeant Taylor!

Later that evening~

Walking back to the barracks, Agnes saw Ella standing by the barracks' door. Wonder what she has on her mind this late in the evening? She seemed like a very likeable young woman. She really admired what they were doing here in England.

"Hi, Aggie, just stretching your legs?" Ella asked.

"Sure, it's a beautiful evening looking out over the low rolling hills and lush green of High Wycombe. It reminds me of Tennessee sometimes. Even though, I'm a long way from home, that's for sure."

Eager to finish their conversation from earlier today, "What's on your mind, Ella?"

Ella began by saying, I was the last one off the plane so there was no one to ask. "Unfortunately, Aggie, I am puzzled by this note I found on the way out of the plane. When I collected my flight bag, this note fell out. Thinking it might be something important, I picked it up and read it."

TOBLUEBOY-

ACASTLEBNEARCGRANTHAMDCAN

EBEFFOUNDGINHCODEIFLYJITKTOL

SWISSMMONDAYNMARCHOFIVEP

ADVISEQCONTACTRONSSUCCESS

TOFUMISSIONVANSWERWISXINY

THEZSMOKE

"What do you think?"

"Ella, it looks like a coded message. Any ideas who sent it? Who do you think it was for?" Agnes asked curious about the note.

Ella shook her head. "I haven't shown it to anyone else but you," Ella stated. "I checked with Lieutenant MacGregor, and she said you were smart and might be able to help me. That's why I showed it to you first. I am keeping this quiet because I don't want to show my hand too soon. I have some ideas about who it could be, but I need to keep my eyes and ears open for some new clues."

"Agnes, you see a lot of the men and women who come into the Mess Hall to eat. Have you seen anything suspicious recently?"

Agnes reflected thoughtfully about anyone who might fit the bill. "No, not at all. I will be sure to listen a little more closely to anything that doesn't seem right." *What could the message mean? Should I tell Cliff tomorrow? He is great with solving puzzles.*

Looking at the slip of paper carefully, she decoded he message for Ella.

TO BLUE BOY

CASTLE NEAR GRANTHAM CAN BE FOUND

IN CODE FLY IT TO SWISS MONDAY MARCH FIVE

ADVISE CONTACT ON SUCCESS OF MISSION

ANSWER IS IN THE SMOKE

Agnes showed Ella the deciphered message, "This is not a difficult code. We had a class in basic code breaking. Okay, look, at the last line of the note it says, "*Answer is in the smoke*," read Agnes. "What an odd sentence. What could that mean?"

"How did you break the code, Agnes?

Explaining how she deciphered the simple code, Agnes explained, "Well, after each capital letter of the alphabet they inserted a word. I just disregarded all the alphabet letters and read what was in between."

Agnes replied, "Is it okay if I tell my friend Cliff? He's very smart and loves to solve riddles and such."

"Well...only if he agrees to not tell anyone else. Can he be trusted?"

"I would trust him with my life," Agnes said confidently. Agnes thought about the sentence she just said to Ella. There were not many people you can trust with your life. Can I trust him with my emotions? Do I want to ignite those old feelings again? I guess I will see as we talk with each other again in the next few days.

Ella smiled and said, "I guess that is as good as one can ask for in a friend."

"Okay, Ella. Also, are there any of your women pilots who could have dropped this message? Any of them who seem secretive or overly inquisitive about things?" Agnes asked Ella finally.

Ella thought about the women on the flight. She didn't know some of them very well. Some of the women were just assigned to the mission a few days ago. She replied carefully, "No one comes to my mind, but I'll give it some thought tonight."

Walking away and back to her quarters, Agnes replied, "Take care, and I'll see you later."

Waving an official looking paper in the air, Agnes said excitedly, "Cliff, my promotion just came through! You may address me as Sergeant Agnes Taylor now!"

Reading the letter that Agnes was waving in his face, "Oh Aggie! That's swell news. You are a wonderful hard-working cook, of course!" Cliff said smiling and hoping for forgiveness for his earlier talk about the dog with Agnes.

"Cliff, I have some unusual items to tell you about and a request for you. Let's put some space between the Mess Hall and lots of listening ears. Okay?" Agnes said quietly as Cliff guided her to the lovely lake area away from the Mess Hall.

"So, what's going on Aggie? What's the secret?" quizzed Cliff. "I'd be happy to help you out." Cliff had always been in love with Agnes and would like to tell her about his feelings for her.

Agnes started, let out a deep breath and shook her red hair quickly. "Lieutenant MacGregor asked me to deliver a message to the RAF Commanding Officer at Harlaxton near Grantham, England. It's north of London. She said to ask for a jeep from the motor pool and take someone with me, so I am not alone. Sound like something you would be able to do?" inquired Agnes. "I don't even know where Harlaxton is located. Do you?"

"Not really, but I can find out. I would love to go with you. I have to request some time off and fill out some paperwork or maybe I can figure some way to run an errand for someone...anyway, I'll do it."

Agnes was relieved Cliff was willing to accompany her to Grantham. He had a keen mind, and they were sure to solve this mystery soon for Ella.

"So, what else is on your mind, Agnes."

"I have had two mysterious things happen since I arrived at High Wycombe. First, Emily and I found an Escape Kit hidden under our duffle bags. You know, an Escape Kit is what personnel who are flying or are dropped into enemy territory have on them, to use as barter with sympathizers. Why would it be dropped with our gear?"

"Secondly, Ella Cook, the woman pilot whom you met the other day in the Mess Hall gave me a note she found in her plane when she arrived. I don't know if there's a connection between these two items. I haven't told my lieutenant or anyone else but Emily about them. I wanted to tell you and see what you thought. I have them hidden in my barracks."

"That's a mystery, for sure. Let me think about it as we walk across the base. I will need to see the note and see what it says. Then, we can make a list of what we know and what we need to find out, and what possible suspects, and ...," said Cliff.

"Wait, a minute, Cliff, this isn't a math problem. I think you'll have more answers when you look at the coded message on the note. Perhaps we can come up with some ideas on the drive to Harlaxton," Agnes said pleasantly. "Okay, the plan is for me to sign out a jeep at the motor pool tomorrow. Lieutenant MacGregor said

I could choose who I wanted to go with me. I'll tell her that you are going with me. Maybe that will clear you with your superiors."

"That's great, Aggie. I will have my superior officer check with Lieutenant MacGregor. Now all the details seem to be settled... it's really swell seeing you after so much time. I have missed you so much. I regret breaking it off with you and leaving home without making things right between us. Do you forgive me?"

"Absolutely, it's okay."

Cliff moved closer to Agnes and took her small hand into his large hand and gave it a kiss. They continued their walk into the misty English air to somewhere they could be alone.

"Oh, by the way, I got a letter from my sister Alice today, and she said Alene and your brother Junior are becoming quite serious about one another. Do you think he will join up too? You know, follow his big brother into the service."

"Hey, I don't know what Junior is up to these days. I haven't seen him since I left home. I think Alene will be a good influence on him though...since she is your sister!"

An idea started to form in Cliff's head as he considered how much fun it would be to see some of London while they were stationed here. Maybe he could try out the idea and see what Aggie thought of spending the day together.

"Aggie, I don't suppose it would matter if we spent the day in London before we went on to Grantham, would it?" Cliff asked. "There are lots of wonderful places to visit...we could see some museums...that would be educational! It would be something you could tell your students after the war is over, and you get your teaching degree."

Giving the idea a few minutes to mull around in her head, "Sure, I think that would be fine, as long as we arrive at Harlaxton in a couple days, and London is on the way to Grantham, I think," Agnes said happily. Agnes thought Cliff's idea to visit London was fabulous!

Crazy! Agnes thought, as she walked back to the Mess Hall. I never thought I would be visiting London. Even though London has sustained a lot of damage during the blitz, there are still places to visit. Not to mention I would be seeing all these famous sites with Cliff. When he left Tennessee, I was sure our relationship was over. Perhaps that flame will be rekindled after all this time.

LONDON, ENGLAND

October 1943

"I feel sure we have no need to fear the tempest. Let it roar, and let it rage. We shall come through."

Winston Churchill

Chapter 9

Two days later Cliff secured permission to accompany Agnes to Grantham. Number 20 Grosvenor Square was General Dwight D. Eisenhower's headquarters in London during WWII. Maybe they should show the message to General Eisenhower's staff? Or perhaps Winston Churchill should be informed since this was occurring on British soil. Churchill's war room was in London. This could be important to the war effort. What should they do?

"Sergeant Ray, I am Sergeant Mark Elderhurst. I will be driving you and Sergeant Taylor to Grantham today."

"Oh really, I thought I was going to drive," Cliff said puzzled. I hope he knows we are planning to spend the day in London. Agnes has her mind set on seeing some of the city and confidentially, we may check in with British Intelligence.

"Well, I have an assignment in Grantham as well. I am meeting with the RAF paratroopers about some training for our troops next month," Sergeant Elderhurst said easily sliding into the driver seat. "Sergeant Ray, you can sit up front with me and Sergeant Taylor in the back please," Sergeant Elderhurst informed Agnes politely.

"Sergeant Elderhurst, Sergeant Taylor and I are also stopping in London for another...eh, assignment on the way to Grantham. It's a secret mission of sorts...is that all right with you?"

"Oh, I think that would be acceptable, Sergeant Ray. I am sure that I can find some suitable activity to pass the time in London. As long as we leave in time to get to Grantham before it gets too late."

"Sure, that will be swell with me," Sergeant Elderhurst added.

Arriving in London, Agnes and Cliff were amazed at the size of the city. It was beautiful even with the recent damage. Crossing one of the lovely old bridges, they could view the River Thames and Big Ben in the distance. Where should they begin?

After Sergeant Elderhurst dropped them off at the nearest Underground, he continued with his plans for the day. Agnes said, "Cliff, this is a terrific idea. There are so many things that I would like to see that I have read about in books. I think Buckingham Palace should be first, and then the Tower of London, Trafalgar Square, and ...." said Agnes excitedly.

"Aggie, we only have one day, not a week! We have to be out of London before lights out and any chance of air raids. So, give me your first choice and then we will see how much time we have left for choices two and three. Okay?"

"Yes, that sounds like you – very logically! I am just so excited to see London. What time are we going to meet Sergeant Elderhurst?"

"He said 1700 hours. So, Aggie, let's get going. I think Buckingham Palace is a great first choice. We can check the tube schedule to see which train we should take." Cliff guided Agnes down the steep steps to the Underground. During the blitz, many Londoners had used the tunnels as protection from the German bombs. They left the tunnels not knowing if their homes would still be intact or a pile of rubble when they returned. This war had to be difficult on families and the children of London. She took a few minutes to think about her own family who had been spared fearing for their lives and homes.

"Buckingham Palace has been spared from destruction by the bombing so far. Hopefully, it will be protected. It is truly a marvelous building and very historical. This is something I have read about since I was little...I can't believe we are actually here, Aggie. The Changing of the Guard will be taking place soon. Then we have to hurry if we are going to Trafalgar Square."

Standing on the train platform, Agnes said, "Okay, here comes our train now. It won't take too much time. Hopefully, we can see the Tower of London," Agnes mentioned happily. "Cliff, this was a great idea. We haven't had an opportunity to catch up since I arrived at High Wycombe. I have really missed you."

Putting his arm around the back of the seat, he said, "I have missed you too, Red. Okay, here's our stop. Get your things. Our adventure is beginning now."

After leaving their second stop, Agnes and Cliff looked at the damage done by the German bombing. There were so many buildings that were destroyed. London would have to do a lot of rebuilding after the war. "Okay, what's next tour guide?" Agnes said hoping they could see a few more places she had read about in the short time they had left here.

After a day of sightseeing, Cliff said, "Aggie, I'm afraid that we have only a couple hours before we meet Sergeant Elderhurst. Churchill's war room is nearby, so we should go there next. This message could contain some sensitive information. Then, we can get a bite to eat at a pub. As they entered the tube station, they surveyed the schedule for the next train to their destination.

Winston Churchill's war cabinet had an underground bunker, many offices, and communications built into a massive reinforced building on Greater George Street. When Churchill described the war offices he said in May 1940, "this is the room from which I'll direct the war."

Arriving at the large stone building where the war room was housed, Cliff and Agnes showed their military IDs and explained briefly what they wanted. They asked if there was anyone from military intelligence available.

They were shown to a small cramped waiting area and went over the message again. After about thirty minutes, an aide came out to inform them there was no one available to speak with them, but if they wanted to leave the note someone could look it over. They declined promptly and began walking back to the tube station.

"Now, we only have about an hour left. What do you want to do, Aggie?"

Thinking it over briefly, "I'm tired. Why don't we go to a nearby pub and relax for a while? We need to save some things for the next time we get some leave! Oh! Cliff, look there is Westminster Abbey! It's a beautiful stone building, but the roof has been damaged. I wish we could go in for just a brief look before going to the pub. OK?" Agnes said with excitement on her face.

"Sure, I never could say no to you – even in high school!" Cliff responded, smiling from ear to ear and giving Aggie a hug.

As they neared the historical old building, Cliff said, "Oh Aggie, it's closed due to the damage during the blitz in May 1941 by a German bombing raid. This sure was a beautiful church and very historic! Hopefully, it can be repaired."

Agnes tried one of the large doors, and it was unlocked. "I think we can just go in for a brief look." The large church doors creaked but opened as they looked in quietly. They could see daylight from the damaged ceiling, but most of the carved wood and burial sites were still intact. Entering the beautiful Westminster Abbey, Agnes said, "Cliff, I want to say a prayer for the troops that are fighting in the Pacific and in France now. I know there's going to be a critical invasion soon, and there will be a lot of men killed. Okay?"

"Sounds like a wonderful idea, Aggie! You're always thinking of other people. I worry about my pilots which I have come to admire. They put their lives on the line every time they fly a mission. They must complete twenty-five or thirty missions before they can go home.

Sometimes they do even more if there aren't any trained replacements."

"Well, Cliff, you do your best to keep their planes repaired and flying. That makes them feel secure that their aircrafts are dependable. You're a fabulous and meticulous mechanic!"

As much as Cliff would have loved to stay here for the rest of the day, he suggested they find a pub and get something to eat. "I'm starved! I haven't had anything to eat since breakfast!" There surely was too much to take in during one visit. Perhaps they could request some more time off before they were sent back stateside.

Cliff said, "Let's go. I'm sure there's a pub somewhere – there seems to be one on every corner."

Leaving the beautiful church, Agnes commented, "Cliff, you're right! There's a pub right there. I think *The Brown Dog* looks like a great place for a late lunch."

After finishing off a late lunch of fish and chips, Cliff remarked, "Look who just walked into the pub, Agnes." As Agnes looked up, Sergeant Elderhurst waved and walked to their table. Their sightseeing was officially over now. It would be on to Grantham to try to solve the mystery that had fallen in their laps.

"Hi, Taylor and Ray, looks like you just finished lunch. I was just looking for some place to get a drink. That's a coincidence finding you two here. I think we will need to leave in about twenty minutes. I'll just head over to the counter and order something while you two are paying your bill," Sergeant Elderhurst said smoothly.

"Agnes, if you need to go to the ladies' room, I will take care of the bill," Cliff offered pleasantly.

Smiling at Cliff and picking up her things, Agnes wanted to be sure Cliff knew how important today had been to her. "Sure, I will be right back. Thanks, for lunch and escorting me around London. I'm sure it's something I will never forget. I'll write my parents and let them know that I had the best tour guide in the Army today! They always liked you, Cliff."

As Agnes left the table, tall and good-looking Sergeant. Elderhurst sat down heavily. He told Cliff he was ready to get going now. "We have a long trip ahead of us, and you never know what types of delays there could be if the Germans decide to do some raids," Sergeant Elderhurst replied grimly.

"We are almost ready. Agnes went to the ladies' room, and I have settled up with the bar maid."

"Hey, Sergeant Ray, how do you and Sergeant Taylor know each other?"

Wondering why Elderhurst was so inquisitive, Cliff answered his questions patiently, "We have known each other for years. We grew up together in Tennessee, and now we are both stationed at High Wycombe. Why?" Cliff asked curiously. Again, Cliff pondered why Elderhurst was so interested in Agnes.

"Oh, no reason, just wondered how you got so lucky to find a good-looking female over here," Sergeant Elderhurst asked Cliff. Cliff filed away his reservations about this man and kept an eye on him as Elderhurst watched Agnes enter the room.

As Agnes came toward the two waiting men, she smiled briefly at Cliff and headed out the door. "After you, Sergeant Ray, I will send for the jeep. It's parked in a secure military lot near Number 10 Downing Street. I have some friends over there," Sergeant Elderhurst said quickly.

Soon the jeep arrived, and the trio climbed in and drove off. "Cliff, look at all the damage that was done to this great historical city. I can't imagine having to go to a bomb shelter or the underground every evening. It must have been terrible for these families."

Sympathetically, Cliff agreed with Agnes, "You're absolutely right Aggie. There is going to be a lot of rebuilding needed when the war's over."

"War is a terrible thing; that's for sure," Sergeant Elderhurst replied grimly. There were certainly many things he didn't like about this war. Hurting innocent people was at the top of his list.

~~~~~~~~

After Ella Cook and the crew left the plane, the secret contact wiggled her slim body through the narrow opening in the floor of the cargo plane. She wanted to slip away from the plane and make her way to Grantham. Her job would be waiting for her after being in Germany for a couple years. The owner always liked her and promised to keep her job open. She would find a place to live in the village and keep watch on the manor.

Getting off the base might be a problem; she would have to use her womanly wiles if she ran into problems.

She would be wise to hide somewhere and wait until dark. She had a face which blended in with others. The Army uniform and forged identification would be helpful.

A Missing Painting

Harlaxton Manor

October 1943

This manor house is located in the English countryside approximately one hour north of London by train. There are 100 rooms, two lakes, and beautiful grounds. It was built in 1837 and housed the RAF Relief Landing Station beginning in 1942.

Chapter 10

"This is beautiful! The long driveway is wonderful. I can't imagine living in a historical castle like Harlaxton. Can you, Cliff?" said Agnes excited to see such an elaborate and luxuriously built manor.

Shaking his head, "Heavens, no! Aggie, have you ever imagined that we would ever visit a place like this? From our humble beginnings, I felt blessed to have a full belly. I walked six or eight miles to my Aunt Vada and Uncle Clayton's house. I remember staying all night with my many cousins, and the next morning Aunt Vada would cook a big breakfast. There were lots of people to talk to with ten kids in the family. I guess I talked a lot and my cousin Glen said, 'I think you know everything' I told him I surely don't know very much some days," Cliff said humbly.

"I suppose I got my love of cooking from my mom. She could feed all of us with just one skinny chicken! Talking about home reminds me of when we were dating. What happened to us, Cliff?"

"Well, I guess at that time I couldn't take on any more responsibility with helping Mom after Dad died of pneumonia. It was a lot for her to manage alone. I never forgot you, my sweet red head."

"Cliff, I have a very important letter to deliver to the Harlaxton Commander, General Stevens, from Lieutenant MacGregor. I should see him before we do anything else."

Agnes thought if there wasn't a war going on, we would be lucky to be here. After realizing what she was thinking, she grimaced and thought, that doesn't sound fair to call ourselves lucky when there are men dying to keep America and Britain safe. Knocking at the massive front door, "I hope we can carry out our mission without getting killed, Cliff," Agnes whispered quietly.

"Don't worry, Aggie. I'll protect my favorite girl! Remember, I'm a trained killer disguised as an airplane mechanic!" laughed Cliff. There seemed to always be a quiet understanding between them that was comforting as they entered the ornate foyer, "Come in and have a seat," the officer on duty said. "General Stevens will be with you in a few minutes. He is taking care of some urgent business and is aware that you have arrived."

Agnes said, "Cliff, look at those beautiful paintings. They must be worth a fortune, even this one that looks like it was smoked damaged in a few places. I wonder why they would have some sorry looking picture on the wall in such an elegant room."

The Great Hall was lined with gorgeous and expensive paintings. The bright sunlight shone through the stained-glass two-story windows. "There must be some reason, Agnes; perhaps it is too sentimental to toss away. People do strange things some time. Actually, they do strange things all the time! This war is a burden to everyone in England. The British have survived the nighttime blitzes for months. It has to be incredible to know you are not going to get much sleep each night because you have to go to the shelter or the underground to protect yourself and your family," replied Cliff. "Our families are lucky they live out in the country away from any danger."

Sweeping into the Great Hall, General Stevens boomed, "I trust you didn't have any trouble finding Harlaxton. I understand that you have a message for me from Lieutenant MacGregor."

Agnes pulled out the message from her purse and handed it over to the general. "Certainly, General Stevens." Agnes was happy to hand over the important paper from the lieutenant. It was a duty she was glad was concluded.

"Thanks, for delivering the message from Lieutenant MacGregor. It's of upmost importance and couldn't be trusted with anyone else. The corporal will see you two to your rooms. After you get settled, dinner will be served in the Great Hall in about an hour. Feel free to look around the grounds or do whatever you want until 20:30. I will have a sealed envelope for you to take back to General Sullivan when you leave in a few days." General Stevens replied secretively. General Sullivan was the Commanding Officer at High Wycombe.

"Thanks, General Stevens," Cliff said saluting and rising to leave. "Yes, thanks so much," replied Agnes standing by Cliff's side and also saluting General Stevens.

The corporal led them to the rear of the manor and showed them to their rooms. "Aggie, meet me outside up on the hill in about thirty minutes, okay?"

"Sure, Cliff, I'll bring the note that I got from Ella and perhaps it will make more sense now that we are in Grantham," whispered Agnes.

~~~~~~~~

Walking around the lovely Lion Terrace gardens Agnes thought how much her life had changed over the last few months. How does a country girl who had never been anywhere end up in England in an elegant and beautiful castle? Agnes turned to see Cliff looking for her. Spending time with Cliff was just the icing on the cake. She had always admired Cliff and what he did for his family. He was also a well thought of airplane mechanic for the Army.

"Cliff, I'm over here by the lions. The lions are guarding the gardens, I think. Aren't they just grand? This entire place is just gorgeous, don't you agree?" gushed Agnes. Even the hotel room in New York City wasn't this marvelous!"

"Whoa, I can only answer one question at a time! Yes, this place is grand and beautiful. I have never stayed in a room this nice before either," Cliff replied happily. "You look beautiful, Aggie."

"Thanks so much, Cliff." Aggie, never one to think she was anything special, replied, "Cliff, I was hoping we could revive our relationship once I was assigned to High Wycombe."

Out of the blue and quite unexpectedly Cliff said, "Well, changing the subject from lions, I think we should get married in February. How about Valentine's Day?"

Agnes had waited a long time to hear these words. She couldn't find a finer man than Cliff who was devoted to his family and faithful to whatever he set his mind to do. Of course, she would have to give him a zippy retort to keep him on his toes. "Don't you think you should wait till I say yes before you set the date?"

Cliff laughed and replied with a quick response, "Oh, yeah. I guess I was getting the cart before the horse...or whatever that corny phrase is - so will you marry me, Aggie?"

Even though she was secretly delighted about the marriage proposal, Agnes teased, "Well, let me see....my February calendar looks clear, unless the Germans get in the way, so YES, I'll marry you - took you long enough to get smart!"

Planting a passionate kiss on Agnes' lips, Cliff said, "You know, I have always loved you!" as he reached for Agnes' hand, Agnes replied, "I love you, Cliff."

After walking hand in hand for a while, Cliff remembered the note, "Okay, did you bring the note?"

"Sure. Here, take a look. I think I have the first part figured out, but I have no idea what the bottom sentence is referring to," said Agnes honestly. "Here you take a look at it."

Taking the note and studying it carefully, Cliff thought the note may not be as important as who was supposed to get this information. What will they do if they know we have it now? I need to make sure Aggie is safe. Whoever was supposed to get this note may want it back at any cost.

Cliff agreed the first part is clearly,

> to blue boy
>
> castle can be found near grantham
>
> fly it to swiss monday march five
>
> advise success of mission luck
>
> answer is in the smoke

What does smoke mean?   Who wrote the message? What about the sentence on the bottom line? There are a lot of things that are in smoke or are smoked, perhaps. This will take some thought and examination. Hopefully, Aggie and I can figure this out soon.

answer is in the smoke

"At this point, I have more questions than answers!" Cliff said confused. "Maybe it has something to do with the chimney of the castle in the note. What castle is near Grantham?   Well, there is Belvoir Castle and Burghley House. Wait! Harlaxton Manor is like a castle, I guess. Perhaps, the note is referring to where we are right now. We could check out Belvoir Castle or Burghley House tomorrow and see if we find anything there. They are just a few miles from here. What do you think?"

"Sure, Cliff, now back to our mystery message; what could "blue boy' mean? Is that a real person or code for someone who works in a castle? We will think about that later – what about "smoke" and "answer" at the end of the coded message?   Seems we aren't very close to solving this mystery."

"Cliff, let's think logically, where do you find smoke - the kitchen sometimes when the cook leaves the rolls in the oven too long or when there is a campfire outside or a fireplace. Harlaxton has several massive fireplaces. I can stand up inside some of them!"

Cliff paused, "Maybe we should divide up the message and focus on a small part of each word. I'll take "blue boy" and Aggie, you take "smoke" and see what we can come up with separately. What do you think?"

"Cliff, you were always so clever solving puzzles in school, I knew you would love this!" replied Agnes. "I heard you sent cartoons and jokes to your Aunt Odessa to make her smile."

"Hey, she's a wonderful lady, and I have enjoyed the newsy letters she has written to me since I've been overseas. Well, I guess we need to get back to the mission. Since we're outside, let's look around to see if anything makes sense out here. It's so beautiful here; it will be a great assignment and lots more fun than patching up B-24s," mused Cliff.

"Hey, the note said something about a mission. I think that sounds intriguing. High Wycombe is a special place with lot of British Spitfires and top brass around. Since it's the VIII Bomber Command to the Eighth Air Force Headquarters, I hope it doesn't involve the safety of your B-24s and P-47s. Britain needs the Spitfires to protect London from the blitz. Cliff, did you see the barrage balloons when you arrived in London?" said Agnes concerned about the safety of the Brits.

Barrage balloons were a series of lighter-than-air bags that were attached to steel cables. The barrage balloons helped to protect the city from aerial attack. The steel cables forced enemy aircraft to fly higher to avoid the cables. The size of the balloons affected the plane's accuracy, thus, helping to protect the citizens of London.

"Yes, Aggie, the Londoners have been through a lot. They are strong people and determined to win this war. English Prime Minister Churchill is a grand leader and knows that the English people will fight furiously to protect their way of life. They are a sterling example to us. They have been fighting since 1939. It's too bad we couldn't talk to someone at Churchill's headquarters. They may have had some information about who wrote the note."

"Guess we better think about the note now. After re-reading the note a few more times, I am convinced Harlaxton is the castle that is mentioned, but why? What secrets does it hold?"

"Tomorrow let's look at the empty greenhouses we saw on the way in this morning near the front of the property. The gardener lives there with his family. He has been here many years and perhaps he knows some of these answers, but we can't let him know why we are nosing around the grounds," Cliff added suddenly.

"Aggie, by the way, I got a letter from my little sister, Cleo, and my mom yesterday. Cleo isn't very old, but she is learning to write well. Mom said my brother Junior is dating your sister Alene. What do you think of that?"

"I guess, your brother has great taste in women! My sister is wonderful and has a sweet spirit. She may become a Ray before I do," retorted Agnes.

I have always loved you!"

"Oh, well, you could have told me..." said Agnes as a grumpy looking man holding garden clippers approached them.

"What do you two want?" Sam the grizzly, unkept looking gardener said sharply.

"You must be Sam. Well, Aggie loves flowers…and we wanted to see if England had some different varieties than we do in Tennessee," Cliff added abruptly.

"Okay, there's always someone snooping around here, and I can't get anything done…alright go ahead and gawk or smell or whatever you want…but don't pick any of them!" Sam added angrily. "Where's Tennessee anyway?"

"Tennessee is in the middle of the United States. Have there been a lot of people coming here recently?" Cliff asked Sam innocently.

"No, I guess not, just that one foreign fella with the bloody strange accent a few days ago. He wandered through my heather and mashed some of my plants. I'm warning you two to be careful where you are walking!" growled Sam sharply.

"Oh, we will be very careful, we promise. What was the foreign man looking for, do you think?"

"He said he was looking for "bluebells" or was it "blue boys: flowers. I have never heard of a blue boy – maybe, it has a blue flower, I guess. Sam grumbled, "people traipsing through my gardens looking for blue plants – nuts!" said Sam as he walked away grumbling.

"Cliff, what do you think that means?" Agnes asked Cliff quietly as Sam walked away. He said, "blue boy" – can it be related to our note? How do we find a strange foreign sounding fella?"

Cliff was musing about what they had seen so far. "We'll keep our ears open, Aggie. Come on. Let's take a look at the heather. Maybe we can plant some when the war's over, and we go home."

When they were out of earshot of Sam, Cliff said, "Aggie, try to look at the heather as a spy might be looking for some clues. That's what I do when I'm trying to solve a puzzle."

After looking quickly at the plants which were a pretty light purple shade, Agnes said, "I love the smell of heather. Maybe that fella was color blind and thinks purple is blue," laughed Agnes uneasily. "Cliff, I don't know what I'm searching for, do you?"

Cliff whispered, "I don't think this guy was a botanist or a flower lover. I do think that a foreign speaking man would stand out here in Grantham. So how does he blend in with so many Brits billeted here? How did he get through security and be able to walk about freely on the grounds?" Cliff quizzed Agnes.

"All good questions, Cliff. I'm afraid I don't have the answers," stated Agnes. "He must be in uniform or have a civilian job that allows him access to the manor without alerting anyone, I suppose."

Cliff had an idea and wanted to ask Aggie about delivery people, "Aggie, you are a cook. Are there any deliveries allowed from local farmers?"

Giving this question some thought she replied, "Well, I guess there could be special government contracts for items that couldn't be secured any other way – like that awful lamb we always have to cook creatively. Ugh! It's terrible," Agnes grimaced.

"Wait! We need to get fresh vegetables from farms around High Wycombe, so I would assume Harlaxton would do the same. Perhaps it was a delivery person, who would not be questioned if he had the correct paperwork or forged credentials. Maybe we should try that idea."

Sam appeared in the doorway of the greenhouse and shouted, "Are you two finished looking at my heather? I need to lock up the greenhouses."

Looking at his watch, "Cliff replied, "Oh, yes. Thank you so much for letting us look over the flowers."

Agnes chimed in, "The heather is lovely."

Sam said, "Well, I had to rush that foreign fella out of here when he started drawing pictures of the heather and the manor from here. He can go out there and draw pictures of the side of the manor!" Sam grumbled sharply.

"Thanks again and I hope we didn't harm any of the plants," Agnes said quickly.

Cliff and Agnes hurried out of the greenhouse area and headed toward the drive quickly, "Well, Agnes. Let's talk again after dinner about what we found out so far."

"Swell, Cliff. I'll get cleaned up and meet you in the Great Hall at 1800 hours. Okay?"

"Sure, Aggie."

Great Hall – 1800 hours

Coming down the gorgeous Cedar Staircase Agnes marveled at the lovely wood and the ornate carving on the sides. Looking up she glanced at the stunning ceiling which included cherubs and ornate plasterwork. She slowly headed into the Great Hall when she saw Cliff admiring the wonderful window overlooking the garden, "Cliff, aren't the stained-glass windows beautiful? I have never seen such luxury, certainly not at my house. Just think of all the ornate and fancy things that could be placed in a house, and they are all here. It's so magnificent."

The staircases are a subject of their own. There are spiral steps, stairs to a blank wall, narrow staircases, standard functional steps, metal steps, carpeted steps, painted staircases, and the elegant and beautiful Cedar Staircase. Some of the staircases lead to nowhere in this elegant manor. There were so many places to hide and to hide things. Many of the rooms have special names – the Gold Room, Minstrel's Gallery, State Dining Room, Great Hall, the Clock Room, and the Conservatory. Many beautifully painted cherubs are on the ceiling of the Gold Room. Many of the rooms have a majestic view of the surrounding country around Grantham.

"Not at my house either, Aggie," Cliff replied sadly. General Stevens was here a few minutes before you arrived and said he won't have the returning message ready for us to take back to High Wycombe for a couple more days, so we will have to struggle along with all this luxury for a while longer. He also told me the background of these historical windows when he saw me admiring them."

"Great! Tell me," Agnes exclaimed moving closer to inspect the coat of arms on the delicate glass. "The man who built this castle or manor put his family's coat of arms in the glass and the names of his family tree at the bottom as well," Cliff pointed to the names below.

Cliff continued his history lesson on Harlaxton, "My dear Lady Agnes, the Great Hall was originally known as the "Baron's Hall." The man who built it was Gregory Gregory. It's no mistake; his first and last name was Gregory. He also put his family's coat of arms and crosses in the marble floor we are standing on here. Mr. Gregory must have been very proud of his family to include them in so many parts of his house."

Agnes glanced at the marble floor and said, "Thank you for the history lesson, Cliff. I know you always wanted to be a teacher. I taught some of the small children at home because they needed some schooling. Oh, it seems people are taking their seats for dinner."

Dinner was served on beautiful china plates with the Gregory coat of arms. Crystal glasses sparkled in the light. "This must be a special occasion or something, Cliff. We are never this fancy at High Wycombe."

Cliff replied casually, "We are having shepherd's pie, mushy green peas, fish and chips, and pudding. I don't believe I have ever had shepherd's pie. What do you think, Aggie? Mushy peas or shepherd's pie, your favorite?"

"Very funny, Cliff. Maybe dessert will be better," quipped Agnes.

After they finished dinner, they headed outside to talk. Cliff remarked slowly, "Aggie, where do you want to get married? I can't believe we are talking about getting married after all these years. After I enlisted, I thought about you and wondered how you were."

"There is a lovely old chapel at High Wycombe and the Army chaplain will probably be available if we let him know soon. I wish our families could be here – especially my twin sisters. I think I'll ask Emily to be my maid of honor. Let's do a small intimate wedding ceremony. I would like a lovely honeymoon somewhere on the coast."

"Bob Marshall, one of the P-47 navigators, was married last month at Clovelly. It's a quaint seaside resort on the northwest coast near St. Ives and St. Agnes. Does it sound like some place you would enjoy? It has your name, St. Agnes, nearby."

"Very clever, Cliff, but I'm no saint!"

"I would go anywhere you are going to be – you know that by now." Cliff moved closer to Agnes, looked around to see if anyone was nearby, and kissed her.

Agnes smiled at Cliff and took his hand. They walked in the lovely gardens, Agnes remarked happily, "Okay, we have planned the wedding and honeymoon in fifteen minutes. I think that is a record!"

"I think I always wanted to marry you, Aggie. It wasn't difficult to plan our lives together."

Now about the note...!" Cliff exclaimed. "I have thought about the smoke sentence a lot and wonder what else could smoke mean?"

As they both pondered what the word *smoke* could mean in the message, she thought back to her days teaching her sisters in the small school in Tennessee. We would write the word and think of all the possible ways it could be used. Maybe that idea would work here.

"Let me throw out some ideas – sometimes people refer to cigarettes as 'smokes' and 'smoke-signals' as in Indians," Agnes said thoughtfully. "Also, smoke comes from campfires and fireplaces."

There certainly are numerous fireplaces at Harlaxton. Maybe something is hidden in one of the lesser used fireplaces. We could check to see what might be in them – besides soot! Sounds like a dirty job, she thought to herself.

"Well, I don't think there are any Indians in England, but there are lots of cigarettes! Could there be a message hidden in a pack of cigarettes and the spy hid them at the manor or the greenhouse?" Cliff said.

"I think we need to go back and talk to Sam, the grouchy gardener. He may know more than he thinks about that foreign man and the drawings he made of the manor. Wait...if he made some drawings, there must be something important around here. Now, let's go to the greenhouse and the walled garden."

~~~~~~~~

The greenhouse and the gardener's cottage were behind a high red brick wall. The walled garden was occupied by the RAF who were doing nighttime trench warfare training. The gardens had been lovely and vibrant during Gregory Gregory's time, but the British troops were wearing down some of the grass and plants. The brick walkways were also removed to allow more space for the men. They assured the present owner, Violet Van der Elst, the bricks would be replaced when they left. The 1st Airborne Division was billeted here during this time. The Royal Army Service Corps – two hundred-fifty Light Composite Company – supplied the division by air. The Dakota, also called a C-47, would fly at treetop level over the field to deliver supplies to soldiers on the ground. American troops were also billeted in the walled garden.

Nearing the walled garden, Cliff opened the gate and shouted hello, but there was no answer. "Let's try the gate in the back, Aggie."

"Cliff, look along the wall; there's a place that looks like someone has been digging outside the wall – like they were burying something perhaps. There are also footprints leading into the woods. What could that mean?" replied Agnes suddenly going over to the wall and inspecting the footprints.

"Aggie let's go to the pub just outside the manor near the main road – I think it's called The Gregory. We might hear or see something suspicious or hear someone talking with an accent. Plus, I'll buy you a drink!"

"Sounds like a brilliant idea – as the Brits say," exclaimed Agnes. "*The Gregory* is an unusual name for a pub. Oh, Gregory is the man who built the manor."

"Just sit anywhere," shouted the bar maid over the noise, as they waited in the pub. "I'll be right with you." The Gregory was crowded with people having dinner or just out for a good time.

"Over here, Aggie," Cliff, sitting down at a table near the back wall, motioned to Agnes, "What will you have to drink?" Cliff asked Agnes after they were seated.

The crowd near the bar were singing a song very loudly, so Agnes whispered her order to Cliff. A very red-faced bar maid came over and wiped off the table and asked, "We have a very nice sticky toffee pudding if you would like to give it a go," she informed the couple, "What will you two be havin' tonight?"

Aggie answered, "I'll have the sticky toffee pudding and some hot tea with lemon. I've become very British since I arrived here."

Cliff said, "I will have the same thing."

After the bar maid left Aggie said, "Do you see anyone that looks out of place? I want to ask Sam Marlowe, the gardener, if he could give us a description of the man who was drawing pictures and searching through the heather. I wonder if these things are connected to each other."

"I'll try to find out if there are any unusual men staying around here. This would be a convenient place for a mystery man to hide out while he stalks Harlaxton Manor.

Look, you can see the manor perfectly from here," Cliff noted.

"Golly, why didn't we think of that earlier? That makes a lot of sense to me. We should ..." Agnes lowered her voice as the barmaid brought their desserts and teas.

"Ay, this is just what you need – our fine pudding and strong English tea, Lass," said the friendly barmaid.

Hoping to get some additional information from the local barmaid, Cliff thought he would ask her about any strange men in the pub. Maybe she would let some information slip about anyone that was new to the area.

"Oh, by the way, where would someone who was unfamiliar with the area find a room around here?"

"Are you needin' a room, sir?" asked the helpful barmaid sweetly.

"Oh, no, not for me. I just wondered in case...eh, I ever needed a room or something," Cliff said quickly.

After the young woman moved on to get someone's order, Agnes giggled at Cliff's bungling attempt at getting information from the barmaid. "Well, that didn't exactly go too well, did it?" laughed Agnes digging into her sticky toffee pudding smugly. "Cliff, try the pudding, it's wonderful – sweet and very tasty. I'd like to try making this dessert sometime...maybe, I'll ask the barmaid for the recipe. See where I'm going with this line of thinking?"

Agnes pointed out, "Women love to talk about their cooking and perhaps, ask a few questions about strange men staying in the village."

After finishing their desserts and teas, Agnes noted, "Cliff, I don't see anyone that fits our description, so why don't we go back to the manor."

Pushing back his chair, Cliff led Agnes out of the pub and onto the street. "Aggie, I want to have another look at the greenhouse on the way back. Okay?"

"Well, I guess it wouldn't hurt anything, but I am getting tired and would like to turn in soon," Agnes said wearily.

Quietly, Cliff and Agnes walked up the drive toward the greenhouse when they heard cries for help. "Cliff, do you hear that? It sounds like someone calling for help. Let's go around to the back of the greenhouse to see where the sounds are coming from."

"Help, help! Sarah, please come help me!"

"Aggie, look! It's Sam and his head's bleeding! Run up to the manor to see if you can find a medic," Cliff said to Agnes desperately.

"Sam, are you hurt badly? Agnes is going for help."

"No, I don't want you to go for help. I can get my wife to bandage my head. Please!" begged Sam.

Taking another look at Sam's head and trying to assess his injuries, Cliff said, "Sam, you are badly injured, and someone should look at that wound. Why don't you want us to go for help?"

"I have my reasons – so please don't let anyone know what happened. Okay?" demanded Sam.

Not wanting to upset Sam any further, Agnes and Cliff agreed to Sam's request. "Okay, we will keep this to ourselves. Can I go get your wife to help you?" Agnes asked finally. "There is quite a large cut and you are losing a lot of blood. Your wife's name is Sarah, right?"

Grateful they had finally agreed to his requests, Sam replied weakly, "Yes, you can get my wife. Just knock on the door and ask her to bring her medical box out here."

Looking at Sam, Agnes thought I wonder why Sam won't let us get some help from the manor. What kind of trouble is he going through? This is very puzzling to understand. He seems frightened more than injured.

"Cliff, I think Sam is going to lose consciousness. I will be right back. Use your handkerchief to slow down the bleeding until I get back with Sam's wife," Agnes rushed to the door and knocked loudly hoping Sarah would answer the door soon. Sam's wound was serious. She continued knocking on the massive door. "Help! Sam's been injured. Hurry!" Agnes shouted at the strong oak door. Why couldn't Sarah hear her frantic calls for help?

Slowly the door creaked open, "What are saying young woman?" the frightened gardener's wife asked softly.

"Sam has been hurt, and he wants you to bring the medical box to help him. He is lying in the back near the greenhouse. My finance` Cliff is with him. Please, hurry!"

After hearing what Agnes was saying, Sarah replied, "Oh, my yes! I will be right there. Please help him until I get there." Sarah rushed inside to get the medical box they kept in the closet.

Agnes turned and ran back to Cliff and Sam. "She's coming with the medical box." Agnes replied when Cliff saw her coming toward them.

"The blood flow has eased a little. There is still a large gash on the back of his head. "What happened to you, Sam?" Cliff asked softly as he cradled Sam on his side to make him a little more comfortable.

Sam's wife came hurrying up the walk and nearly fainted when she saw Sam's ashen face. "I didn't see anyone – just felt this blow to my head and then everything went black."

"Sam, why can't we call for the doctor or a medic at the manor? I think this could be a serious cut on your head," Agnes told Sam desperately.

"No! Promise me you won't tell anyone about it," Sam said quickly to Cliff and Agnes.

"Okay, Sam we will keep this quiet for now, but we are stopping by tomorrow to check on you again. Aggie let's get Sam to his feet and into the house," Cliff added softly to Agnes.

After getting Sam settled on the sofa and leaving their house, Cliff said, "Okay, let's head back to the manor and forget about this incident for tonight. We'll add this to the other things we don't know about the note, Escape Kit, and now this attack on Sam. What could it mean, Aggie?"

"I don't know Cliff, but I'm getting a headache trying to sort all this out in the dark."

As they reached the door to the manor, Cliff said, "Hey, my sweet red head, try to get some sleep, okay?"

"Absolutely! I am very weary after this day's events," Agnes laughed uneasily. "I just wonder what's going to happen next! Good night, Cliff." They both saluted the guard at the entrance to the manor and went inside.

"Cliff, where is your room?" Agnes inquired. She wanted to know where he was if there was another unexpected emergency.

"Downstairs and to the right. Where is your room, Aggie?"

"It's upstairs on the second floor which looks out on the garden. I'll keep my eyes open," Agnes replied sleepily. "Well, maybe not that open, until tomorrow."

"I'm still perplexed about why Sam didn't want anyone to know what happened to him. What could be going on with him? I hope he isn't seriously hurt. Clearly, he didn't want our help. We can check on him early tomorrow after breakfast."

"Sounds like a great idea."

After walking Aggie to her room, Cliff said, "After what happened to Sam, we can't be too careful. Sleep well, love," Cliff kissed Aggie and walked away softly.

She got ready for bed, reviewed all the events of the day, and tried to make sense of what they had uncovered. Working with Cliff was wonderful. He had a very calming way of making the facts make sense to her. Even as tired as she was, it was difficult to quiet her mind and fall asleep. Perhaps tomorrow would be the day they solved this mystery.

Later that night…Gardener's Cottage behind the Walled Garden

"Sarah, pack a few things you can carry safely. We must leave tonight. The American man and woman are asking a lot of questions. They won't quit until they have figured out our secret. Hurry, we must go quickly before we're missed."

"Yes, of course, Sam."

"Sarah be brave. We must go far away from this place."

In the meantime, Sam put some money and a few clothes in a small bag. Looking at the photograph, he wondered what went wrong with their daughter. How could she turn her back on her country and her parents? They may never know the answer to this question. There would be no reason to take the picture along with them.

Even though his bandaged head throbbed, the couple moved carefully through the secret tunnel to the gatehouse by the manor drive. This tunnel was not known by many people. In the pitch-black night, they moved silently away from the gatehouse unnoticed. Looking back, but seeing nothing, Sam wished things could haves been different for all of them. They would have to leave Harlaxton behind forever.

The next morning…

Breakfast at Harlaxton Manor

Agnes wrinkled her nose and said, "Cliff, what is this? It appears to be some type of sausage, but not like anything I have ever eaten. Have you tried it yet?" Agnes quizzed Cliff about the plate of food in front of her.

"Hold on a minute, I can only answer one question at a time. I understand it is blood sausage. It's pork…how bad can it be? Right?"

"I'm not sure I want to eat anything that starts out with blood…! I saw enough of that last night on Sam's head. I want to go over there as soon as we can. Maybe they have some oatmeal and fruit I could exchange for this sausage," Agnes whispered to Cliff.

Cutting a small piece of the sausage, Cliff said, "Aggie, where is your sense of adventure? You may want to add this delicacy to the menu at High Wycombe. Yum! Very tasty!"

"Somehow, I don't believe you are eating that meat. It just doesn't smell like something a human should be eating. I'm heading to the kitchen to see if there is another choice for breakfast. I'll be right back, and we can get going."

After ten minutes Agnes returned, "Cliff, I was talking to the Mess Sergeant, and said I would trade some of my recipes for some oatmeal and raisins," Agnes beamed.

Before they could leave the dining hall, there was quite a disturbance in the hallway outside. Suddenly, the lieutenant in charge of operations at the manor stormed into the breakfast area. His face red and angry, he boomed "Has anyone seen the charred painting of Harlaxton Manor that was over the fireplace in this side room? A very valuable painting is missing from this secure area, and I need answers now! I mean if this building isn't protected how can we expect to keep security of more important information housed here for the sake of the crown and all that's holy! Someone, please tell me they saw something last night. I have reports to make, and I don't have any information to go on!" He ranted on for about five minutes.

Quietly Cliff offered to the lieutenant, "I think we could help you, lieutenant. Could we talk in your office?"

"Sure, let's go to my office and see what you two know about this. Follow me."

Cliff and Agnes followed the lieutenant down the hall and into a small cramped room that was supposed to be an office of sorts. Boxes of stationery and stacks of papers lined the walls and an ornate chair sat beside a beautifully carved mahogany desk, obviously very old and extremely valuable. "I'm Lieutenant Butler, and I'm in charge of the possessions in the manor as well as several other assorted duties. I'll have to account for the disappearance of this particular painting to the general. This is not something I am eager to do without some answers for him."

Looking at the pair of American soldiers before him, he wondered how they could be mixed up with this theft. They didn't look the type.

"So, what can you tell me about it, Sergeant? By the way, who are you two and why are you here?"

Eager to explain how they were involved with the missing painting; Cliff began detailing how they happened to be at Harlaxton. "Well, I am Sergeant Cliff Ray, and this is Sergeant Agnes Taylor. Sergeant Taylor was on a mission to deliver a message to General Stevens. We are waiting for a return message to General Sullivan. Agnes and I are stationed at the base at High Wycombe. We are working on decoding a message about a castle and Grantham and who might be trying to get some information from here. I can only assume the painting is tied to the message we have been working on since we arrived. We haven't really seen anyone who looks suspicious. Why is the painting valuable to the manor?" Cliff said interested in why the lieutenant was so upset about a scorched painting of the manor.

The lieutenant seemed like a pleasant middle-aged man. He began patiently explaining the value of the painting to Cliff and Agnes. "Well, the painting is one of the few things left in the manor that belonged to the original owner. Even though it doesn't appear to be a valuable painting, it is. It was placed above the fireplace in this office and now it's missing. I was supposed to watch over it and guarantee its safety to the present owner. Now, I must tell the general, and it's probably a demotion for me. So, you think someone broke into the manor and was looking for the painting because of its value or is there another reason someone would want it? It wouldn't be because it is so beautiful, I would imagine," he laughed softly.

"We have a couple thoughts on its disappearance, perhaps it contains a secret message on the painting or behind the painting or maybe they want to sell it and send the money to the Nazis. What would the value be on the black market, lieutenant?" Cliff said.

"It's difficult to say. Perhaps, a hundred thousand pounds would be a close estimate I suppose," Lieutenant Butler said.

"That would be a boost to the Germans now," Agnes softly replied to the men in the room.

Looking over at Agnes he thought she was a very smart woman to make that connection so quickly. "Well, Lieutenant Butler, we will keep our eyes open and let you know if we see or hear anything about the painting."

"Lieutenant Butler, there was another incident you may want to investigate. Sam Marlowe was attacked last night. I don't know if these two things are related or not." Cliff reported.

"Thanks, Sergeant Ray. I will check on the information you have provided, and I will also let you know if anything turns up. When are you leaving the manor?" he asked Cliff and Agnes.

"We don't know...whenever the general gives us a return message, I suppose," Agnes replied. Agnes and Cliff got up to leave and proceeded to the garden as they had originally planned. At the time Cliff felt as if someone was watching them leave the lieutenant's office.

Arriving in the garden area, Agnes started the conversation logically by asking Cliff, "So, what do we know for sure? The information about the note, the suspicious activity last night with Sam, and the Escape Kit from the first day I arrived in High Wycombe."

Cliff and Agnes continued their conversation about Sam and what he had to do with all the goings on at the manor. "I don't think we know anything for sure except that Sam is hiding something. We decoded the message, but don't know what it means. The Escape Kit is still a mystery, and the mystery man is still on the loose. A seemingly ordinary scorched painting is missing. Does that about sum it up?" Agnes asked.

Cliff nodded his head in agreement and went over to look at the courtyard. Some paratroopers were talking about the Alan Williams turret, a steel copula that defends the manor. Two men use a machine gun to take care of any problems that we might have with the enemy," Cliff said suddenly. He thought of all the lives lost already. Surely, our Allies, such as the Brits, must be weary of fighting by now.

"Let's go on to the greenhouse now. If that's okay with you, Aggie."

As they approached the greenhouse, Cliff questioned "Aggie, let's check the back of the cottage first. I want to see the area where we saw digging before we talk to Sam. Could our mystery man have buried something and came back to get it last night? Maybe that is why Sam was hit over the head. Perhaps he saw too much."

"Just as I suspected, the dirt has been moved and raked over this spot by the fence. Look! That rake has blood on it. I think the intruder used it to hit Sam," Cliff said bluntly. The pair continued to look around the area for any other clues that would be helpful in finding a suspect who could have hurt Sam or stolen the painting from the manor.

Cliff, after knocking on the door repeatedly, noted, "Aggie, I think Sam and his wife are gone. Possibly, they have left the manor. Look in the window. There are clothes thrown around the room and some pictures are missing from the wall over there. What do you make of it?"

"Well, I think that Sam and his wife are mixed up in this whole mess somehow. His wife seemed like such a nice lady, but Sam was not very friendly even before he was attacked," Agnes replied. She remembered seeing how upset Sam's wife was when she heard that her husband had been injured. Then Agnes told Cliff when she awoke this morning there was some noise in the room overhead. She wondered if someone was hiding up there. It is sure possible with all the secret tunnels in this manor. Why would someone be rummaging around about 0300 hours this morning? Maybe we need to ask ourselves – what is so valuable in this place you would need to creep about in the wee hours of the early morning? Could it be the painting? Agnes thought to herself and tried to add up the information they had accumulated in the last few days.

"Cliff, there are lots of valuable items in this place. Let's see - there are statues, vases, stained-glass, and priceless pictures. So, the stained-glass would be hard to take out the front door without arousing suspicion – agree?"

Cliff laughed, "Sure, Aggie. I guess the statues and vases are valuable to art collectors and smugglers, but maybe it's not what is valuable, to a spy or double agent. It's a theory worth investigating."

"Cliff, there seems to be something that's worth getting caught or worth fighting for in this manor."

Agnes thought to herself; I think there are more clues hidden in these thick walls. Thinking of what Lieutenant Butler had told them earlier in the day, she wondered where someone hide a valuable picture of the manor or themselves?

Cliff responded, "I have a hunch. Some of the paratroopers were talking about the secrets of Harlaxton, and there are at least a half dozen secret tunnels or passageways in the manor. Also, there are secret doors and hidden rooms. A paratrooper said he heard someone could go into a tunnel in the Conservatory. That would be a handy place to get away with valuable items. Let's check that one first since it's nearby and may be easily accessible."

Heading to the back of the manor, Cliff and Agnes looked around the walls and floor looking for an entrance to the underground tunnel. "Cliff, look at the beauty of this room. There are marble and floral designs at the base of these columns. Everything is so fancy here." As Agnes moved a large potted palm, one of the corporals rounded the corner and looked at her oddly. "Did you lose something Sergeant Taylor?" he inquired.

"Oh, no, I was just admiring this fine palm tree. It is surely a lovely plant. Don't you think, Cliff?" Agnes asked quickly hoping she didn't look guilty. They would have to be more careful with their search for the secret tunnels.

Cliff picked up her line of thinking and quickly added, "Yes, you are correct. It would look great moved a few inches to the left. You have such an eye for design and how things should be arranged. Yes, that's much better."

The corporal looked skeptical but left them to the palm plants shuffle. "Oops, that was close, but I did find the entrance. It's that door near the palm tree over there. Do you think we should both go, or should one of us stay here and watch for snooping corporals?" Agnes said worriedly.

"I suppose you're right Aggie. I will go down there, and you relax here and think of some logical reasons we would be hanging out here. I'll be right back - I hope!"

Cliff was gone about forty-five minutes. Agnes was beginning to worry and tired of looking like she belonged there. Finally, Cliff returned quietly to the Conservatory where Agnes tried to look relaxed whenever someone walked through the room. "Cliff, I'm so glad you're back. What did you find down there?"

Coming over to sit beside Agnes, Cliff whispered, "Well, I didn't see anything suspicious. Definitely, no valuable paintings or spies in that particular tunnel! Lots of spider webs though. I walked about two hundred yards and didn't see anything that seemed helpful. So, I came back up and peeked out before coming out. Did anyone ask what you were doing lounging around here?"

Checking the entrance to the Conservatory first, Agnes replied, "No. Everyone seems to be busy or engaged with someone else in the manor. Even though the coast is clear here, however, I did see these heavy cast iron grilles that are set into the floor. I think it is a way to heat this room. This is an amazing room with the glass ceiling which would warm the Conservatory when the sun is shining. Someone had a wonderful knowledge of gardens and how nature works. By the way, could the grilles in the floor be a way to access the tunnel below this floor?"

Inspecting the grilles from a distance, he thought a slim man could get in and out of the grilles unnoticed. "I don't know Aggie. I would need to have more time to investigate and remove these heavy grilles. That's an idea though."

Taking a few minutes to catch his breath, Cliff said, "Also, there is the railway tunnel where the coal is brought into the manor. I understand from the guys that the people who work here use coal wagons to deliver the coal to different areas of the manor. You know there are lots of fireplaces at Harlaxton. Since Harlaxton is located on a hill, the tunnel is on level with the third floor of the manor. There are lots of possibilities with that tunnel."

Cliff thought to himself: we need to look at the coal railway tunnel. There could be clues there we hadn't even thought of. Who do we need to ask? Or do we risk asking anyone? We don't want to tip our hat that we are on to someone.

"That's certainly something to ponder."

"Aggie, by the way, have you heard from General Stevens? How much longer do we have to collect information about the note and the picture? We will have to go back to High Wycombe soon. As much as I love this manor, it certainly has a lot of oddities."

"I think it is time for dinner. I will look for the general's aide and see if he has any ideas about when we are to leave here. We will try to investigate after dinner, but I don't think we should ask anyone yet. I think we can look around ourselves to see if we can find the tunnels. If we fail, then we can ask."

Agnes thought I'm sure eager to find this person...hopefully, sooner rather than later. As I recall the note said by March 5. I don't know if we can solve the puzzle that quickly.

After dinner…

After a satisfying dinner with the other staff stationed at Harlaxton, the after-dinner conversation turned to how the war was progressing and how long it might be before the Allied were able to defeat the Nazis. After a respectable time had passed, Cliff and Agnes said their goodnights and proceeded to the sunroom to continue their earlier conversation about the mystery they had become involved in.

Lieutenant Elderhurst was sitting at a table with the present owner of Harlaxton, Violet Van der Elst, and General Stevens. They were laughing at an outrageous story Mrs. Van der Elst was telling with gusto. She moved to her Kensington home when the RAF came to the manor. Sometimes she came back to visit and to check on the house. Often, she had made new purchases for the estate when she traveled.

After the general excused himself, Mrs. Van der Elst asked Elderhurst, "Would you like to have a drink, lieutenant?"

"Certainly, I would like that very much. Lead the way."

Mrs. Van der Elst led Elderhust to an elaborate and ornate room nearby. "Violet, this is a beautiful room. The ceiling is very lovely too. You have impeccable taste in furnishings and have a great eye for art. I hope it's okay to call you by your first name?"

"Please do. Here is your drink, lieutenant."

"Some of the guys were talking about secret tunnels and passageways in the manor. Is there any truth to it?"

"Why yes, there are many secret doors the servants use to deliver meals and supplies to different rooms. I understand there are a few tunnels too. Why do you ask, lieutenant?"

"No reason. I just found it fascinating – just like you, Violet!

"Why, thank you. This room is very nice, but I prefer my private room upstairs where I hold my seances. It's much cozier than these large drafty rooms on the first floor.

You must attend some time. Many people are interested in visiting their dear departed loved ones. My late husband, John, died in 1934, and I want to talk with him sometimes."

"Oh, sure. Well, the Army keeps me very busy, so I don't think I would have time to join you."

"I understand. It's not for everyone, I suppose. When I'm in London I am kept very busy with my different interests. Would you like another drink?"

"No, I really need to go now. Thank you so much for the drink and conversation tonight. Have a good evening."

Elderhurst left the lovely room and shook his head. What an unusual lady he thought to himself. There aren't any dead people I want to talk to.

~~~~~~~~~~~

"Cliff let's see if we can find the railway tunnel. It must be off from the third floor. Perhaps, it's in the back of the manor which is the way it looks from the outside. I walked out there this morning to see if I could find anything from the outside. I think it is in the southwest corner of the manor. Let's go upstairs and see if anything seems like a likely place for a door or maybe a dumb waiter that would hold coal. Maybe there is a map of the tunnels somewhere. Sound like a plan?" Agnes explained patiently.

"Yes, it sounds like a plan, but Aggie, don't go snooping around by yourself! It is dangerous for a woman to be alone with this spy or agent or whatever this person is."

Agnes couldn't believe Cliff didn't consider them equals. Sometimes Cliff could be so over-protective. Firing back at him, "Is that so! I'm a trained U.S. Army personnel, I'll have you know, Sergeant Ray!" Agnes replied indignantly.

Feeling the heat coming from the fired up red head, Cliff said, "Yes, I know, Red. Pardon me if I care what happens to you! It is just a suggestion that we stay together and try to figure this out. Okay? I didn't mean anything by calling you a 'woman'. Am I forgiven? We don't have a long time before someone wonders what we are doing or where we have gone," Cliff explained patiently.

"Sure, let's get going now," Agnes said climbing the stairs ahead of Cliff. "Okay, Cliff, I think it should be close to this outer wall. Perhaps nearer to the back."

Cliff opened several of the doors near a set of stairs. "Aggie, I think I found it." Opening the door for Agnes to enter, Cliff's eyes began to adjust to the darkness.

"Cliff, I think you're right. I can feel cool air coming up this way. Also, the walls are rough like a brick wall. Look! There are candles and matches on the wall on the next step." Agnes lit a candle for each of them and a couple spares for when the candles started to go out.

"Let's go slowly so we don't fall or make a lot of noise and alarm anyone," Cliff whispered quietly.

"Cliff, I am right behind you. I smell some damp air as well. Can you see anything ahead of you?"

"Well, so far all I can see is coal dust from where the servants would have brought in the coal for the fireplaces. I don't know when they would have stopped or if they are still doing it now. I'll check with some of the staff to see how the manor is heated. Does it look like anything has been disturbed or if anyone has been down here recently to you?"

"Well, it's hard to determine without some detective work and some time to check out things closely. We don't have a lot of time unless we give up eating and sleeping!" Agnes remarked.

The candles only illuminated a small area around Cliff and Agnes. Holding up his candle, Cliff was able to see a large wooden door at the end of the tunnel. The tunnel was very old and must have been built in the 1850's. There were large brick arches and brick vaults in the doorways. There were several coal chutes along the side of the tunnel walls. Those chutes must be used to deliver coal to the different rooms of the manor. Also, there was a square door cut into the ceiling of the tunnel. It was large enough for a person to climb out of onto the roof above. Could someone use this tunnel to come into the manor unnoticed?

Proceeding on down the tunnel, Cliff was looking for anything that looked suspicious. He thought he saw something ahead. Looking down, he picked up three cigarette butts, a stub of a pencil, and some scraps of paper that had been left behind, Cliff pondered what he had found, "Aggie, looks like someone has been here recently. Also, there are footprints and some pieces of paper that have been ripped up. What do you make of that?"

Agnes carefully looked over the cigarette butts, the stubby pencil, and the paper, wondering what they might mean. Clearly, someone was surprisingly cognizant of the many tunnels of Harlaxton. Either they had been here before or they knew someone who had. She thought, maybe it was someone who used to live here or perhaps work here. Perhaps someone was thinking of another plan or was writing a letter to someone else...maybe, they were writing another message.

"It's difficult to read what is written on the paper without glue to put it back together. The paper is shredded, so I don't think that's possible either. I will put the pieces in my pocket, and we can see what we can do later," Agnes explained to Cliff as a puff of wind suddenly blew out the candles, leaving the tunnel completely shrouded in darkness. It was a cold dark dampness that sent shivers down Agnes and Cliff's arms. Cliff couldn't see his hand in front of his face. He had to protect Aggie...but, he couldn't see her.

"Aggie, where are you? Aggie, Aggie!" Cliff whispered as quietly as possible. He thought we need to get out of here now! Reaching out his arm to try to locate Agnes, he moved along the tunnel wall. Using the rough brick wall, Cliff moved to his right. He stumbled over Agnes suddenly. That uneasy feeling was back again. Who could be in here with them? Cliff thought without panic.

Someone had been hiding in the shadows watching them try to read the shredded note. The hidden person seized this opportunity to extinguish Cliff and Agnes' candles. When it was totally dark, that person was able to escape. Perhaps they entered the tunnel through the square door in the ceiling. This person was very familiar with the railway tunnel.

Agnes called out desperately, "Cliff, someone was in here! I felt someone push me down, and I heard some footsteps running away. Then, I must have passed out briefly." Agnes felt her head for a bump. Yes, there was a small bump on the back of her head. "It's not bleeding, and it doesn't really hurt. So, let's get out of here for now."

Cliff considered what had just happened and thought, we may be on to something. What was someone doing in here? Whoever it was must have run past us in the dark.

"Why don't they want us down here?" Agnes asked nervously.

"A good question I don't have the answer for! Yes, Aggie, I think we have done enough for one evening. Hold on to me, and we will follow the wall up to the stairs."

"Cliff, something just flew over my head!" Agnes screamed. I can't stand this place! What could it have been? I felt a brief wind and then I knew something was there. I could smell it too! It smelled like an animal. Could birds get in here, do you suppose? I don't like being in here! Agnes mulled all these things over as they stumbled toward the entrance in the inky darkness.

Thinking this excursion was taking a treacherous turn, Cliff took Agnes' arm gently and said, "Let's try to find the opening before something else happens."

After a few feet, Cliff saw a tiny sliver of light coming through the door ahead of them. Someone had left the door open. Relieved they had chosen the right way to get out of the tunnel, Cliff said, "I know I shut this door when we came down here. Aggie look up at the ceiling! I think I know what else was down here with us!" Cliff explained. "Those are bats! They won't hurt you, but they are certainly scary when the lights are out. They are probably just hibernating or looking for something to eat. Luckily, for us they don't eat humans! Ready to go?"

"You bet I'm ready to go now! Come on Cliff!" Agnes rushed to the door ready to be rid of the bats and the unknown human. "Look, Cliff, there are footprints from the coal residue on the floor by the door. There definitely was someone else in the tunnel. By the size of the footprint, I would say it was a man's shoe."

Cliff thought to himself, this has just become more dangerous. He said reassuringly, "Let's keep our eyes open and see if anyone has coal dust on their shoes. There's someone who doesn't want us to find the painting, but they don't know how determined we are to get to the bottom of this. Come on, Aggie, let's go."

Harlaxton Manor

Grantham, England

October 1,1943

Twenty-six-year old Skye Marlowe dialed the phone hoping her contact would answer quickly. They had to wrap up this problem and conclude the mission soon. The future of the war depended on what happened in the next two days. Skye's future was at risk if her contact didn't follow orders.

Chapter 11

"Hello, I hope you can talk for a few minutes," she whispered quietly looking around to see if anyone was nearby.

"Yes, but why are you calling me here. I don't know if anyone is around or listening. What do you want?" He said irritated that she would call to check up on him.

"I have been trying to find the note. I accidently left it on the plane and didn't discover until too late that it was missing from my pack. How much do they know about our plans? Both she and Sergeant Ray are smart – it won't take them long to figure out the message and what it means to the Reich. The March 5 deadline date is not possible now. We will keep trying to get the painting out as soon as we can. Take care of them if you have an opportunity," Skye told him bluntly.

"I will try to make an opportunity, but they are almost always together. Perhaps, there will be some 'accidents' that are going to occur to Sergeant Taylor and Sergeant Ray in the next couple days," he replied grimly.

"They are so shrewd! Tonight, they found the railway tunnel and some things that I left behind. I'll have to be more careful from now on. I have the painting stashed away and waiting for the right time to get it out of the manor. There is usually someone on duty or walking the halls here. I don't think Taylor and Ray have a clue about me. I'll get things cleaned up here. I promise."

"Do what you can from your end. Try to call me when you are free. Remember there will be serious consequences if this mission isn't completed. There is no turning back now. You understand?" Skye reminded him pointedly.

Nervously he thought, she didn't need to tell him what he had to lose because he had become involved with her. Perhaps he should have thought this through a little more carefully. It didn't matter now; it was too late.

"Sure, sure, I know what's at stake here and what happens if I'm discovered. Not pleasant. I have to go now before someone wonders who I'm talking to at this hour. Don't call me again! I will call you when I know something. Okay?" he said impatiently. "I'll take care of it soon. I'll try to make sure they don't return to High Wycombe but if they do, someone will have an accident. I'll have a plan in case that happens."

"Fine. Just remember what I just said about turning back! It won't be pleasant for either one of us if Berlin sends for us."

Skye hung up the phone and wondered if she had made a huge mistake picking him for the mission. The success of the rest of the war depends on that painting. She had taken many risks and could lose everything if he didn't do what she told him to do. They had to get the painting to the assigned meeting place. What would she tell the Germans if they failed? Their lives were at stake.

The Threatening Message

Harlaxton Manor

October 1943

Chapter 12

"Okay, Aggie, we have the return message to deliver to General Sullivan, so after breakfast we go back to base at High Wycombe. Can you have your bags packed in a couple hours?" Cliff asked Agnes.

"Sure, I will go to my room now, get things together, and meet you for breakfast. I am sad to leave Harlaxton as it's such a lovely place, and we haven't solved all the pieces to the mystery yet. Sure, we can't stay a few more days, Cliff?"

Smiling at Agnes, he quipped, "As much as I would like that too, we have orders – remember we are in the Army!"

"I'll find Sergeant Elderhurst and let him know we are leaving after breakfast. I have already packed my gear and made some notes for us to discuss when we get back to High Wycombe. Sorry, I can't help being so logical! I know that's what you were going to say. I know you so well!"

Agnes decided to take one last walk around the lovely grounds and garden before meeting Cliff and Sergeant Elderhurst. Agnes thought, this has been such a beautiful place to spend some time with Cliff. Too bad there was this unpleasant situation with Sam Marlowe and the messages to solve. This would be a swell place we could enjoy together.

Agnes thought, I wish I could tie all these loose ends up about the mysteries that have occurred recently. There must be an explanation for all the things that have happened. What are we missing?

After eating breakfast, Agnes returned to her room and collected all her gear. She gave one last look around the exquisite rooms and all the splendor that defined Harlaxton. Is that a letter on the dresser? Walking over to pick it up, she saw an envelope with her name printed in large letters. Opening it, she read the single page –

'DON'T PUT YOUR NOSE IN THINGS THAT DON'T CONCERN YOU! GO HOME. FORGET WHAT YOU FOUND. IT WON'T BE HEALTHY FOR YOU TO CONTINUE.'

Apprehensively, Agnes folded the letter and put it in her pocket. She left the elegant room and went to look for Cliff. Should she show it to him or forget it? She never could keep anything from Cliff. He always knew when something was upsetting her.

Agnes saw Cliff coming toward her with his travel bag. This threatening letter had certainly put a damper on her good spirits. Trying to smile and seem lighthearted, she remarked, "Let's try to come back here again someday, Cliff."

"Sure, Aggie, we'll certainly try."

On pins and needles, Agnes considered her options. They had been in this together from the beginning, so there really wasn't any other choice. Pulling the letter out of her pocket, she shoved it into Cliff's hand quickly, and looked to see if anyone was nearby. He read the threatening letter and looked at her shaken. He didn't want anything to happen to her. She was his world now and always would be. They would have to evaluate how important this mission was to them when they got back to base.

After breakfast, Sergeant Elderhurst brought the jeep around to the front and helped Cliff and Agnes load their gear in the back. "Okay, Sergeant Elderhurst, I think we have everything we need. We're ready to go."

"Fine," said Sergeant Elderhurst brusquely as he started the engine and climbed into the driver's seat, then waited for Agnes to get settled. Agnes gave a long sad look at the manor as they pulled away. What were they going to do about the threatening note? Should they take it seriously? This part of the mission was becoming very frightening. This was something to discuss with Cliff when they got back to base. Next stop, High Wycombe.

Merry Christmas to All!
High Wycombe, England
December 25, 1943

Light snow was falling over the grounds of the once Abbey Girls School making the countryside look like a winter wonderland. Sadly, not many miles away there was still a war waging over the German farmlands.

Chapter 13

Even though Agnes and Cliff had returned to High Wycombe, they hadn't had the serious discussion about the mission yet. It was easy to put it out of one's mind while preparing for the holidays. After Christmas they would need to consider bringing Lieutenant MacGregor into the mystery.

Coming out of the kitchen, Agnes said cheerfully, "Midge and Emily, are we ready for the Christmas rush today? I want this to be special for the guys. Sometimes we forget that some of these guys are just kids, barely eighteen or nineteen. It must be tough to be away from their families for the first time. So, whatever we can do today will be appreciated."

After the Japanese attack on Pearl Harbor in December 1941, guys all over America rushed to join the service and fight our enemies. Within a few days, the United

States had declared war on Japan and Germany. Patriotism was at an all-time high.

"Sure thing, Aggie," said Emily. "I have the special Christmas cakes ready to put in the oven. Midge is doing the eggs and bacon. We will be open for business in about thirty minutes. Okay?"

"Sure, girls, you always come through. I am getting the tables ready with the paper cutouts we did yesterday afternoon and peeling sweet potatoes for dinner today. We will just have some simple sandwiches for supper since many of the guys will have the day off, unless the war decides otherwise!"

"Aggie, there are some new girls coming in to help for the simple dinner meal this evening. As you know, Ruth and I have an overnight leave to spend Christmas with my family. Since I live nearby, the family really appreciates that we can come home for a few hours. Are you going to be okay without us?" Midge asked anxiously.

"Surely, Midge, you are so sweet to be concerned...but, I will be fine with a few extra girls and the guy on K.P. tonight to help out in the kitchen. Please go home and enjoy some time away from here. Now, where is your home?"

"Oh, my home is in Huntingdon which is about an hour north of London. We will catch a train in about an hour to head home." Since Ruth lives too far away for an overnight visit, she was going home with Midge this time. Midge's family always has a big meal on Christmas Day. There are ten children in Midge's family. With rationing it hasn't always been easy for her mom to keep all the kids fed.

Looking more cheerful for the girls' sake, Midge said, "I'm looking forward to seeing my boyfriend, Geoff, too. It has been nearly a year since we have seen each other. He's in the RAF and hasn't had any leave. We'll be thinking of all of you back here. Thanks, and Merry Christmas, Agnes," Midge said with heartfelt affection.

"Is Huntingdon a small town, Midge? I don't believe I have ever heard of it before."

"Yes, it's a small town where everyone knows each other and looks out for their neighbors. Sounds like where Cliff and you grew up?"

Suddenly, getting homesick for her family, Aggie brushed her emotions aside and replied brightly, "Of course, that does sound like Red Boiling Springs. Everyone knowing your business often is a pain, but it usually works out for people though. Have a wonderful Christmas, Midge. I'll see you when you get back to base. Be sure to tell me about your Christmas dinner and what you did with your family," Agnes replied and walked away quickly.

Midge and Ruth turned to leave, but not before placing a small package on the prep table for Agnes. "Midge, let's go before Aggie returns to the kitchen." The girls all agreed that they wouldn't give each other gifts, since they didn't have a lot of money. "I don't want her to fuss at us for giving her a Christmas present, but I wanted her to have something special since she is away from her folks this year."

"Right thing to do, Midge," Ruth responded quickly.

"It's time to leave now." Ruth pulled Midge through the back door and off they went to catch their train.

After leaving the girls and walking out of the kitchen, Agnes put out the meal trays and silverware just as the first hungry airman walked through the door.

Cliff said sheepishly, "Sorry, I'm so early but I have a busy day. Those banged up airplanes don't know it's Christmas Day. I do want to see you later this afternoon if you are free, Aggie. What do you say?"

Always eager to see Cliff, she responded, "Sure, I can make some time for you, of course. General Eisenhower said all the troops were to get a special Christmas dinner today. We are planning a special noon time dinner which includes all your favorites – ham, sweet potatoes, carrots, green beans, homemade rolls, pumpkin pie and apple pie. So, you better show up no matter what you have to do!"

"Hey, you bet I'll be here! Regulations say that we get to eat no matter what needs to be done in the hangar!" Cliff said, reaching for a tray and proceeding to get his breakfast of bacon and eggs.

As things in the kitchen got hectic, Agnes lost sight of Cliff, thinking of seeing him later to exchange presents. Returning to the kitchen for another stack of meal trays, Agnes spotted a small package on the prep table. What could that be...the girls and I agreed not to exchange gifts? Agnes picked up the package and looked at the tag. "*To: Agnes.*" Ripping off the colorful paper, Agnes looked at the small black and brown figure of a dog. The figurine looked just like Frankie. Agnes said laughing out loud, "Those girls are just impossible!" She thought I'll place it in the kitchen window so Frankie can watch us work.

One of the guys stuck his head in the kitchen and yelled, "Hey, we need some meal trays out here." Agnes grabbed some trays and quickly headed out the door with a smile on her face. She enjoyed cooking and was so fortunate to be surrounded with such wonderful women.

Later Christmas Day~

One thing about the Army, they always got the mail through even though there was a war going on. Going to mail call, she was fortunate to hear her name called and received two letters today. It was going to be a wonderful Christmas! The first letter was from her mom who had written a short but informative note about the family. The second letter was from Alice, one of her sisters, who really gave details about her friends, who was home from the war, and who had just been drafted. After reading the latest news from home, Agnes ran a comb through her dark red hair and straightened her uniform. She wanted to look nice for Cliff.

Looking down, she realized she missed a letter addressed to her with no return address. It's probably a Christmas card from one of her friends in Tennessee or maybe from Vera. Opening the envelope, she saw it was a single sheet of paper. It was another threatening note.

Back off from your detective work or you will regret it. Tell your boyfriend too. You could get hurt if you don't stop now.

Merry Christmas

Well, isn't that a mean-spirited Christmas letter. I'll bring it along to show Cliff. Maybe it is time to discuss whether to continue or confess to our superiors. Aggie hated to give up on solving the mystery.

Strolling through the now dead and dried up gardens, Cliff saw Agnes walk toward him carrying a package. "Merry Christmas again, Cliff. It's extremely hard to Christmas shop when you can't get off the base very easily, but I did manage to find something I think you will like. Open it!"

"Well, I want you to open your present too!" Cliff handed a small square box to Agnes and smiled at her.

"Gee, Cliff, what do you have here? Hmmm, maybe it's a new potato masher...or a knife for the kitchen...or maybe, I'll just open it and see!" Agnes said delighted that Cliff had remembered her.

She liked to tease Cliff, and he did the same to her. "Open it, Agnes, it's not a kitchen tool...for Heaven's Sake!"

Opening the small box, Agnes wondered what Cliff had picked out for her, "Oh! Cliff, it's beautiful! When did you get this lovely ring?"

"Oh, I have my secrets. I thought you should have an engagement ring."

"I think it's just wonderful! Thank you so much!" Cliff slipped the ring on Aggie's finger and kissed her tenderly. He admired the diamond ring and looked forward to when they would be married. "How does it look, Cliff?"

"It looks as pretty as you are!"

"Cliff, thanks so much! Open your gift now."

"Sure, I'm going to. What could it be...I know a new wrench...or parts for that engine I'm having trouble getting back together...or maybe a whole chocolate cake just for me to eat!"

One of Cliff's best features was his sense of humor. True to form, he saw the humor in every situation – except maybe, the coal tunnel at Harlaxton. Bats weren't humorous!

"Very funny!" Agnes replied. "I hope you like it."

"Oh, Aggie, this is terrific! Where did you find this pocket watch? It is so finely made. It's just great and thoughtful of you, as usual. I don't mean to sound ungrateful, but I know you don't make a lot of money. You send home money like I do."

Agnes explained Mrs. Clarke had some financial problems and wanted to sell the watch for some cash. "She's the one who took Frankie when we had to find a place for the dog. I told her I would be happy to just give her the money, but she insisted that we must make a trade. She wouldn't hear of it, so I bought this watch from her." I hope that keeping the evacuee children hasn't been a financial burden for her family, Aggie mused.

"I thought it was beautiful! I'm so glad you like it. You'll have no excuse for being late, not that you are ever late though."

"I'm sorry for Mrs. Clarke's financial problems, but I do like the watch a lot. I love you, Aggie." Cliff took Agnes' hand in his, and they walked down to the lake hand and hand.

Cliff remembered the Christmases he had back home. The family always had a big dinner, and then they would visit the rest of the relatives and the nearby neighbors. There were never a lot of gifts under the Christmas tree, but the Rays had each other and lots of love to go around! Aggie and he would have many more great Christmases together when they returned home.

"Gee, I wonder what the folks are doing today. I wish we could call them. Letters just aren't the same, and it takes so long to get a letter here too. This war won't last forever."

"Aggie, this has been a wonderful Christmas! I'm sorry for the soldiers in the battlefield. God bless them all."

"Oh, speaking of letters, I received this one today." Not wanting to spoil this happy moment with Cliff, she reluctantly pulled the note out of her uniform pocket. She shoved it into Cliff's hand and bit her lip.

"What's this, Aggie?" Gauging the look on her face, he knew it wasn't good news. Cliff read the note and put his hand on Aggie's shoulder gently. "What do you want to do about this problem?"

Aggie frowned and said grimly, "I don't want anything to happen to either of us, but I would like to see this though to the end. I know we can solve this mystery given enough time. I hate to lose!"

"Okay, Red. I will do whatever you want, but I must admit this scares me. I don't want anything to happen to you before you become Mrs. Ray. My mother would never forgive me." Cliff said trying to lighten the mood. They agreed to give their detective work some more time to uncover more clues. Cliff only hoped they weren't making a huge mistake.

~~~~~~~~

When her staff returned to base, Aggie smiled and hugged both young women. "Welcome back. How was your leave?" Midge replied for both women, "It was quite nice to spend time off the base." Ruth's face, however, wore the expression which said everything was not good.

Aggie noting something was very wrong, said, "What's happened, Ruth?"

"When I called my parents to wish them a Merry Christmas, they said my brother-in-law was arrested by the Nazis while in Norway. Of course, my sister is very upset."

"Why was he in Norway?" Agnes asked puzzled about how this could happen.

Ruth explained, "Rolf was born in Germany, but his family moved to England in 1933. They could see the direction the country was taking as Hitler gained control. Rolf was trying to get his cousin out of Norway when they were detained. My sister is very frightened. Our family is trying to get a message from Rolf's friends in Oslo. It's very difficult now."

In 1939, Norway declared itself to be a neutral country when Germany began its plan to take over countries in Europe and surrounding areas. "German troops invaded Norway on 9 April 1940, planning to capture the King and the Government to force the country to surrender. However, the Royal Family, the Government and most members of the Storting were able to flee before the occupying forces reached Oslo."

Aggie didn't know how to help. Unfortunately, this was happening often to families. She had heard reports of what was happening to Jews and gypsies. Many of the pilots had mentioned to Cliff the destruction their bombs had caused in Berlin and Frankfurt. Nearly seventy percent of Berlin had been destroyed. This was madness!

The Hangar

High Wycombe, England

January 1944

"...the base (High Wycombe) was a "nerve centre" for the United States 8th Air Force Bomber Command in World War Two."

Chapter 14

"Cliff, I need a crescent wrench. Have you seen an extra one around here? I can't imagine what has happened to mine. They do have a way of walking away," Mac inquired of Cliff.

"Well, I haven't seen an extra one, but you can borrow one of mine. I thought you scheduled a flight to get your extra hour and ten minutes for this month's flight pay."

"Oh, I do need to do that today. I'll get it done now. Thanks for reminding me." Mac walked over to the corporal who scheduled the planes. "What planes do you have going up today so I can get my flight hours?"

The corporal replied, "I have two planes scheduled for flights today. Pick one."

"You just put me down for one of them, corporal. It doesn't matter to me."

Explaining to Mac it was against regs for him to make the decision, the corporal said, "No, I can't do that; you decide which plane you want, Mac."

After some thought Mac replied, "Okay, I'll take the one leaving at 1600. I'll be ready." Walking back to tell Cliff he would be gone for a couple hours, Mac grabbed what he needed and headed for the plane that was leaving soon.

Cliff saw him coming and yelled to Mac. "Hey, Mac, you have a letter that was just delivered. Smells like it's from your wife. You might want to come pick it up!"

Quickly, Mac made his way over to Cliff, took the letter and opened it immediately. Mail from home was a treasure and Mac wanted to know what Ruth had been doing at the hospital in Terre Haute where she was a nurse. "Ruth says they are seeing some of the vets coming back from the war. There are some terrible injuries, and she prays that we are all safe here. Well, there's more of course and some of it is personal – not for your ears, Cliff! I'm scheduled to take a flight in about ten minutes, so I'll see you later."

Three hours later~

Scanning the sky, Cliff looked for his friend's plane over and over. They were late returning to base, and he was very concerned for Mac and the pilot. Ten more minutes - he walked around the tarmac again trying not to be too stressed. Then he spotted a plane to his right coming in for a landing. Hopefully, it was the plane Mac had hitched a ride on earlier in the day.

As the plane landed with a thud, Cliff walked out to greet the crew. "Everything go okay, guys?" As the crew departed the plane, Cliff saw Mac slide out of the door and look under the plane. "Mac, how was your ride?"

Mac finished his exterior inspection and walked back to where Cliff was standing. "Hey, everything went well, and I was just checking the cowling and the wings to see how they stood up during the test flight. The engine sounded fine so no problems to report. Why are you out here instead of working on the engine you started this morning?" Mac inquired as he looked at Cliff's long face.

"Well, I wanted to tell you before you heard it from someone else. The plane you didn't choose for your flight today crashed into the ocean on its test run, and the crew didn't survive. I'm sorry, Mac, that could have been you. In other words, you chose the correct plane. I'm so sorry for the guys who didn't make it."

Mac looked ashen and bowed his head for a few minutes. "Gee, I'm so sorry for their families. Look, thanks for telling me. I think I need to go back to the barracks and write a long letter to Ruth. It's been quite a day. Then, I will get that wrench you promised me and finish working on the engine I started this morning. See you later, Cliff. I appreciate hearing the news from you." Cliff put his hand on Mac's shoulder as he solemnly walked away.

"Let me know if I can help, Mac."

The Wedding

High Wycombe, England

February 23, 1944

Chapter 15

"Aggie, we have passes to go to town to get our marriage license, or as it is called in England – Wedding Registration. I'm sorry we couldn't schedule the wedding for Valentine's Day. The only open day was 23 February. Are you disappointed?" Cliff asked anxiously.

"I'll never be disappointed as long as we can be together, Cliff. The 23rd will be wonderful. Can the base chaplain perform the ceremony?"

"Sure, the chaplain said he was delighted to marry us. I have been working on the honeymoon details too. My lieutenant said the historic Red Lion Hotel in Clovelly was a wonderful place to stay. It's on the coast with those large rocks along the retaining wall. It was built in the 18th century. Sounds interesting doesn't it, Aggie?"

Cliff was always thinking of her and what she would like. He was going to be a wonderful husband. She was glad she had decided to join the WACs and was sent to England.

"Sure, Cliff. It sounds lovely." She thought, I was hoping to see more of England while I was stationed here. It is a beautiful country that has been at war much longer than we have.

"The lieutenant said there were beautiful views and the area is very quaint. I want it to be a nice wedding for you since your family won't be here. I know how close you are to your sisters," Cliff said patiently.

Letters were an important part of the soldier's life in the military. It was not possible to call or to come home as much as Agnes would have liked and, of course, it was impossible for our families to come to England. We'll have many grand stories to tell the folks when we are discharged from the Army.

"I wrote my mother a letter explaining that we are getting married in February. She wrote back that she understands, and we could have a family get together when the war's over, and we come home. I know she and my father are disappointed, but they understand how we feel about each other," Agnes said. "What about your family, Cliff? Do they understand about the wedding?"

"Sure, they just want us to be happy. My mom is fine with it."

As they were leaving the base and going into town to get the marriage license, Agnes remarked, "Cliff, I didn't know your middle name was Delano? How could I know you all my life and not know that about you?"

Laughing, he explained, "Well, there's an explanation for that, Aggie. The military requires a middle name, but I didn't have one. So, I made up one. President Roosevelt has a very nice middle name – Delano – so, I thought if it's good enough for our president, then it's good enough for the U.S. Army!"

"Cliff, I don't believe you! That is so funny and patriotic!" Agnes laughed.

There were lots of details to take care of even with a very small wedding. Both Agnes and Cliff applied for and received a week's furlough for their honeymoon. The Army was very understanding of their situation. Hopefully, the Germans would be too!

The wedding day ~

"Well, the big day is here, Aggie. Are you nervous?" Emily asked happily.

"Heavens no, Emily, I've known Cliff all my life! People back home always said we were made for each other. Of course, there weren't too many fellas to pick from in Red Boiling Springs, but from what I have seen in the military, he's still the best! Emily, thanks for standing up with me today. It means a lot to me to have you nearby."

Emily added, "I wouldn't miss this wedding for the world! So, you will wear your dress uniform and a white carnation corsage?" Apparently, fancy flowers are difficult to find in February in England Emily thought without stating it to Agnes. Aggie was a beautiful bride and as happy as she hoped to be some day.

For all Emily's outgoing spirit, she longed to have a special guy like Cliff. Even though she was over the moon happy for her best friend, she wished for her own special day.

Agnes stated sadly, "Well, since I won't be wearing an elegant lacy white wedding dress...I guess it's the only thing that will be white today."

Ruth opened the door slowly as she didn't want to interrupt any important prewedding conversations. "Mrs. Clarke brought you a lovely present for your wedding. She grows flowers in her greenhouse for special occasions." Ruth produced an elegant bouquet of lovely purple heather and white daisies."

"Oh my, they are just perfect! Heather is one of my favorite flowers." Aggie smelled the bouquet and couldn't quit smiling.

"Aggie, you look divine! A simple ceremony suits you both. The chapel is very historic and a lovely setting for a military wedding in England. The sun is shining brightly. What more could you ask for today?" Emily exclaimed.

"My family to be here with us, I suppose," Agnes replied sadly as a single tear slid down her cheek. I need to stop thinking about what I don't have and be excited about what I do have! What a silly goose I am today." She forgot about her sad thoughts and looked at Emily.

"Oh, Aggie. I'm sorry I was rattling on and upset you. Sometimes, I open my mouth before I think."

"No, Emily. It's not as if it hasn't been on my mind for days, but the important thing is that Cliff and I will finally be married. Now, we can officially solve mysteries together – like Nick and Nora Charles of the *Thin Man* series at the movies. I just love those two!"

"Oh, yes. You mean Myna Loy and William Powell. She was always dressed to the nines. I love their clever banter with each other. Hey, it's a lot like Cliff and you!" Emily laughed.

~~~~~~~~

As the small stone chapel filled with their friends, her maid of honor walked down the aisle with Agnes following closely behind her. "Ladies and gentlemen, will you please stand," the Army chaplain said gently.

The wedding ceremony continued with these words, "Agnes Taylor, will you take this man to be your wedded husband?" The chaplain repeated to Agnes who happily said, "I do."

Cliff looked devotedly at Agnes, as the chaplain repeated the same vows to Cliff. "Clifton Delano Ray, will you take Agnes Taylor to be your wedded wife?" Cliff said, "Sure will." Everyone laughed, "Oh, I mean, I do."

After sharing their first kiss as husband and wife, Cliff and Agnes walked down the aisle as everyone stood and clapped. "Cliff, I am so happy!"

"Aggie, I knew we would one day be together. It just takes me a long time to get it right, I guess," Cliff said humbly. A friend took some pictures, so they could send them home for the family.

Mac offered his congratulations by shaking Cliff's hand and giving Agnes a hug. "Cliff, I hope you and Agnes are as happy as my wife Ruth and I are."

Next, Midge, Ruth, and Emily rushed up to hug both Cliff and Agnes as they walked back down the short aisle of the church. "We are so excited for both of you! Have fun and don't worry about anything in the mess. We will take care of everything!" The girls said together.

"Yes, that's what I'm afraid of with you three in charge of the menu!"

Midge replied, "The ceremony was absolutely brilliant! Well done, Cliff and Agnes. Well, we have a surprise for you two. The girls and I have baked a traditional British fruit cake for the small reception next door in the small anteroom attached to the church. We know you didn't have time to plan anything special, so we wanted to give you two a bloody good send off!"

"Oh, Midge, thanks so much! That's wonderful!" Agnes rushed to give Midge a huge hug before being led to the anteroom for the small reception. In the reception area, there were tables of small cakes, petite sandwiches, and punch. In the center of the table was a huge vase of the same heather and daisies as her bouquet. "When did you girls have time to put all this together? It's just beautiful! Cliff and I so appreciate it. It's a lovely reception. Thank you so much!"

After the reception, Cliff and Agnes were anxious to be on their way to Clovelly. Mac, Bob, Midge, Emily, Ruth, and the rest of their friends followed them out to the jeep and continued their well wishes with the American tradition of throwing rice. Walking down the weathered stone steps, Agnes said, "Hurry, Cliff, I am getting pelted with rice. I think some of your buddies are enjoying getting back at you! They are throwing it like baseballs...except they're hitting me!" Agnes exclaimed.

Stopping at the jeep, Agnes turned around and tossed the bouquet. When she looked back at the group of women gathered on the chapel steps, Emily was holding the bouquet.

Cliff opened the jeep door and helped Agnes inside. Some of the pilots had tied empty tin cans to the back of the jeep. Ruth and Emily had made a sign that said, **"Just Married"** and placed it on the front of the jeep. "Okay, Aggie, we are off on our next adventure!"

"I can't wait, Cliff!" exclaimed a radiant Agnes.

Bob was taking them to the train station and off they went with lots of cheers and laughter from their friends.

~~~~~~~~

Someone was watching the happy couple leave in a stream of rice and cheers of good luck. Maybe they wouldn't need so much good luck, if they had kept their noses out of other people's affairs. "They had better watch out!" he whispered angrily.

~~~~~~~~

"Thanks, Bob, for the ride to the train station. You may want to take the cans and the sign off before you head back to High Wycombe!" Cliff told Bob, a navigator and one of Cliff's best friends.

"I don't know, Cliff. I might like the attention!" Bob laughed easily.

Cliff and Agnes gathered their bags and headed to the station. Bob drove away with the cans clanking and the sign flapping in the breeze. "Bob is a great guy and has completed thirty missions over France and Germany. He should be going home soon. He needs a long rest after all the missions and destruction they have done to the Axis powers," Cliff told Agnes.

"Cliff, there's our train. Hurry! We don't want to miss this one today. Our special day!" Agnes laughed. "I like to ride on the British trains. They're always on time, and you don't have to drive on the left-hand side of the road. We can both sit back and relax! We should be at Clovelly in about two hours I should think."

"Cliff, it's been a perfect day. What a nice wedding and reception. I didn't have any idea what the girls were up to. It was such a wonderful surprise!" Laying her head on Cliff's shoulder Agnes closed her eyes and began to drift off to sleep.

Cliff wondered about the coded message and what it might mean to the war. He had a new responsibility now, and he must keep her safe. Was solving the mystery worth putting themselves in danger?

After an hour, Cliff gently touched Agnes' shoulder saying softly, "Aggie, wake up! Don't sleep through our honeymoon!" Cliff joked easily holding Aggie hand. "I don't want you to miss any of the beautiful scenery."

They rode along the English countryside looking at green fields and small streams. There were miles of pastures filled with cattle and sheep.

"Aggie, we are pulling into the station at Clovelly."

Cliff pulled their luggage together as they prepared to leave the train, "Cliff, after we get registered and settled in our room, let's have someone take our picture down by the water. I want to send some pictures home for our families."

"Surely. Anything I can do to make you happy. Whatever Lady Agnes Taylor Ray would like, I will try to make possible...always!" Cliff said planting a kiss on Agnes' nose.

Agnes stepped down from the train and waited for Cliff to point out the way to the hotel. It was just a short walk. When they arrived, the happy couple stared at the historic and quaint hotel. Cliff always knew what she would like. "Cliff, I love it! I wouldn't want to stay in a fancy hotel...the Red Lion Hotel is the perfect place!"

The Honeymoon

Clovelly, England

February 1944

The Red Lion Hotel sits near the harbor in Clovelly, Devon. Clovelly was originally a fishing village.

Chapter 16

"Aggie look at the ocean! The rocky coast is a wonder! I'm taking a mental picture to describe it to my brother Junior. I'm not sure words are sufficient to describe how marvelous this place is to us."

"Cliff, I am so happy! We are going to have a glorious and exciting life together!" Agnes said lovingly.

"The Red Lion Hotel has been on this spot since the 18th century, and it's a terrific place for our honeymoon. Let's check out the dinner menu. I'm starved after the ride here on the train."

Walking up the rocky path, Agnes remarked, "I am wondering about the missing painting at Harlaxton. I am still pondering why that particular painting would be taken. As I remember it wasn't very brightly colored, but maybe it's not the painting itself, but what it means to someone else, perhaps. Any ideas about how they got the picture out of the manor?"

"Well, we checked the sunroom tunnel and the coal tunnel. It would be easy for a man or a woman to slip through."

Recalling the bump on her head and the scary bats Agnes responded, "Oh, those bats in the coal tunnel! How could I forget that tunnel! It was very creepy in there! Cliff, you said woman. Are you thinking we are looking for a woman instead of a man? I don't think we should rule out a woman...since we really don't know who it is – yet! Do you suppose there was a clue from the message painted into the picture? Or maybe a secret written on the back of the painting. What do you think?"

"I think, I'll have the Shepherd's Pie, Aggie!" Cliff laughed trying to lighten the mood.

"Oh, Cliff! I'm serious about this!"

"I know, Aggie, but it is our honeymoon. Let's take a break from crime fighting for a few days!" Cliff replied easily.

"What if the trail gets cold while we are enjoying ourselves...?" As the waitress approached their table, Agnes responded, "I haven't looked at the menu. Go ahead, Cliff, give me a minute."

"Okay, I'll have the Shepherd's Pie and hot tea."

"I'll have the fish and chips and hot tea. I'll think about dessert. We are celebrating a special day today...our wedding!" a beaming Agnes replied.

"Congratulations!" the waitress replied smiling. "We get a lot of newlyweds here. I'll bring you a special dessert."

"Oh, that would be great! Cliff, listen to that song. Isn't it *Begin the Beguine*? I love that song!"

"Well, Aggie, then we should dance. Brides should dance to their favorite song on their wedding day! Don't you think?" Cliff smiled happily at Agnes.

"Okay, I think that is a great idea, but as you remember, I am not a great dancer."

"I don't care how you dance; it's a good excuse to put my arms around you for a while without worrying about saluting a general or something!" Cliff teased. Cliff took Agnes' hand and led her to the small dance floor. Other diners started to join them as the song played. "This is just like old times together back in Tennessee, Cliff, our being together and enjoying just doing simple things."

After the bride and groom finished their dance, the waitress delivered hot, delicious food to their table. "Aggie, don't you just love eating at our own little table without hundreds of GIs looking at us! The view of the ocean is just outstanding at sunset!"

Unable to shake her uneasy feelings, Aggie shared her thoughts with Cliff.

"Cliff, it is wonderful, indeed, but I keep feeling like someone is watching us – no, not the hundred GIs from High Wycombe! It is just a feeling I have that I can't shake."

"Aggie, you worry too much! I think there is a wonderful dessert headed over here!" The waitress sat a decadent looking plate of small rich and creamy chocolates and fresh strawberries in front of Cliff and Agnes.

"Cliff, there is nothing better than chocolate to celebrate, don't you think?"

~~~~~~~~

Carefully watching Cliff and Agnes from the shadows, another person mused, following Agnes and Cliff here was not a good idea. There is no place to hide. I'll stick around for a day or two and head back. Where could they have hidden the note? How am I going to get her away from him? I am running out of time.

~~~~~~~~

The next morning ~

"Good morning, Mrs. Ray. I love you so much! I'm so happy you decided to marry me. Ready for breakfast, Red?" Cliff asked pleasantly.

"Yes, I'm ready for breakfast. I was delighted to marry you, Mr. Ray." Agnes put her arms around Cliff and kissed him. This was a wonderful honeymoon.

"It's great I don't have to cook for a few days. What are we going to do today? Any ideas?"

"What about a hike up the hillside and out on the rocks? There are probably some beautiful views down the coast. We'll have to be careful with all the sharp rocks and steep cliffs off the coast. How does that sound?"

"Sounds wonderful, Cliff!"

Cliff took Aggie's hand, and they walked to the eating area downstairs. After they had eaten a hearty meal, Aggie said, "Breakfast was delicious...just like dinner last night. Those eggs were very orange instead of the yellow ones we have at home. I am ready to begin our adventure." Agnes followed Cliff down the stairs to the coast and all the rocks.

"Aggie, the view is spectacular. I have been thinking about the painting and what the spy could want with a smoke damaged painting. Isn't it just an old castle? Is there something special about it? I remember seeing it before it was stolen and wondered why they would keep it on the wall. There are so many other wonderful items in the manor."

Obviously, we are missing something...what about Sam? Where could he have gone so quickly? Could he have been hiding somewhere on the grounds? Again, we have more questions than answers, Agnes thought carefully going over the events of the last few months in her mind.

~~~~~~~~

Returning to their hotel room at the Red Lion, Cliff opened the door to let Agnes enter. "Cliff, look at our lovely room! It's been ransacked!" Agnes exclaimed.

Their belongings were scattered around the room, and all the dresser drawers were hanging open.

Cliff pulled Agnes back into hallway, as he looked inside the room to make sure no one was still inside. Giving her the go ahead, he said, "Aggie, be careful! It looks like someone has been digging through our bags. What do you think happened? Did we leave the door unlocked?"

"Cliff, I remember you locked the door before we went down to breakfast. You are always so careful. Is there anything missing?"

"I don't know. Let's look around, and then we should inform the hotel staff to see if anyone else has had any problems," Cliff replied quietly.

Cliff didn't want to frighten Aggie, but he thought it was time to leave. It was oblivious to him someone was watching them. He would suggest a new location to continue their honeymoon. "Tomorrow, we are going to visit St. Agnes, in honor of you and your namesake. I have done some research, and it sounds like somewhere you would enjoy, Aggie."

"Cliff, I hate to leave this lovely historic old hotel, but I'm ready to explore some more of this area. It has been a wonderful honeymoon so far except for the ransacked hotel room."

After checking with the manager, Cliff told Aggie, "No one else in the hotel has reported any problems."

"Do you think it has anything to do with the missing painting and the note?"

"It's hard to say, Aggie, there didn't seem to be anything missing. I've rented a car today, so we can have some freedom of what we want to see. Plus, I think we need a change of scenery. Are you ready to go?"

"The manager told me that the views are stunning in St. Agnes. The area is in Cornwall, and it should be a beautiful drive! Then we can walk along the unspoiled beach for a while before lunch. Sound like a good idea?" Agnes gave Cliff an overview of the area as he was driving them along the curvy roads going to St. Agnes.

Agnes continued, "The cleaning lady said St. Agnes was once a center for mining copper and tin until the 1920's. Since it's along the coast, of course, it's another quaint fishing village."

 "Should I call you St. Agnes since you are an expert on the area? You are pretty and nice, but you're not old! Twenty-four is really not old and quaint...yet!" Cliff joked.

Leave it to Cliff to make a joke, Agnes thought joyfully. "Ha, ha! Let's stop and walk for a while, Cliff."

"Sure, I'll look for a place to pull over. Okay, up ahead there is a place to park. We can do some hiking over to the left and down to sparkling blue ocean." Cliff opened the door for Agnes and took her hand.

After about an hour, Cliff stated, "Aggie, I think we better head on over to St. Agnes. I am getting hungry, and we still have quite a few miles to go. These curvy roads are slow going for someone not used to driving on the other side of the road!"

"Sure, that's fine with me. This fresh sea air is so relaxing. I won't want to go back to High Wycombe and all the problems we have to solve."

As they approached the car, Cliff noticed that the car looked peculiar. After closer inspection he said, "Aggie, we have two flat tires! I wonder how that could have happened. I checked everything before we left. I hope there's a spare in the trunk. One flat I could understand, but two flats. Someone is following us or trying to keep us on edge."

"I agree with you, Cliff. What are we going to do?" Agnes said scanning the area for anyone to help them. They seemed to be on a particularly deserted part of the road.

"Perhaps we should look in the trunk, or the boot as the British call it, to see if we have any spare tires. Who can we call for help do you suppose?"

Just as Cliff opened the trunk, a speeding car headed toward the car. "Aggie stay back!" shouted Cliff as he grabbed Agnes and dove for safety. After brushing themselves off, Agnes asked, "Cliff, are you all right?"

Cliff pulled Aggie close to him and could feel her shaking. When she was calmer, he gave her another hug and released her. "Yes, but a little shaken for sure. Okay, this is becoming serious. Maybe we should inform the authorities or our superiors. Perhaps this is getting out of control and not a game for us to solve any more. What do you think Aggie?"

"I don't know," Agnes stubbornly replied.

Agnes thought, I have to admit that scared me quite a bit, but I don't want them or him or her – whoever it is to win and think they scared us into quitting! I don't want Cliff to know how upset I am about this 'accident.'

Still concerned about Aggie, Cliff asked shakily, "Did you see what kind of car it was or who was driving?"

Reflecting on what just happened, Agnes said, "Well, not really, but It looked like a dark blue car, Cliff. I was just trying to get out of the way! I really didn't see anything for sure that I remember other than the color. Whoever was driving was certainly coming straight at us. I don't think it was an accident, and they didn't stop to see if we were okay. So, I think we can conclude it was deliberate," Agnes replied.

"Okay, for now, but I don't want anything to happen to you...let's check on the tires."

"Cliff, I know you are an ace mechanic, but can I help you do anything? Find the jack or unscrew something?"

"No, really, I will have them done in five minutes if you don't help me!" Cliff laughed.

She could always depend on Cliff to see the funny side of an unpleasant task. "Very humorous, Sergeant Ray! I'll just sit over here and look beautiful then," Agnes replied.

"You are beautiful, you know. I can't believe we are married. This is a fine way to start our new life together. Aggie, I am very concerned about what just happened."

Looking in the trunk, Cliff was relieved to see two replacement tires stowed there. He could solve this problem easily, since he could replace the flat tires, and they could be on their way. Cliff urged Aggie to stay away from the road in case the car returned to make another swipe at them.

In a short time, Cliff had the tires changed, "Aggie, do you have anything I can wipe my hands on? I'd like to get cleaned up before we continue."

Agnes promptly replied, "No, Cliff. Maybe we can stop at the next pub or somewhere that has a restroom, or loo, since we are in England."

Stopping by the next pub, they pulled into the parking lot and turned off the engine. "Aggie, I'm going to the restroom to clean up. Would you order a sandwich and some tea for me?"

"Sure." Agnes found a lovely table by the front window where they could watch the car as they ate lunch. They didn't want anymore 'accidents' while they were inside the pub.

Cliff returned to the table, "Looks like a great place for lunch. What kind of sandwich did you order for me? I'm starved!"

"Well, I ordered a chicken sandwich with crisps for you and a ham sandwich for me. I hope they are serving something good for dessert too." After devouring their lunch, they headed to St. Agnes without any further incidents.

"Cliff, did you tell anyone where we were going for our honeymoon? I was just wondering how the person in the blue car knew where we were going, if it was an accident, which I don't think it was. I only told Midge, Ruth, and Emily we were going to the Red Lion Hotel. Of course, they don't wish us any harm; however, someone is following us."

Thinking over Aggie's question, Cliff responded, "I only told Bob who I would trust not to blab to anyone else. That's an interesting perception, Aggie. I hadn't thought of that angle."

"Well, another thought is someone has been following us since we left the base. I will try to be more observant of who is around and what cars are behind our car. That brings up another question, Aggie. Do we tell our superiors when we return to High Wycombe or keep it to ourselves – that's the dilemma."

Agnes looked perplexed, but replied with a smile, "We can decide later. Right now, I want to enjoy the rest of our honeymoon. I think we have waited long enough to be together."

Arriving at St. Agnes, Agnes observed, "Cliff, look at the beautiful village. It is stunning! I can't wait to do some hiking and walk along the beach. The beach reminds me of my days in basic training and Daytona Beach...many miles away from here. The waitress, where we ate lunch, said we should visit the St. Agnes Beacon as you can see the landscape in the area.

"I would love to have some fresh fish for dinner. Being so close to the ocean, it should be delicious!"

"Sounds great! Oh look, Cliff, there's the St. Agnes Bakery where I'm sure there are some great cookies and pastries! What a lovely place! This was a terrific idea."

"Okay, Aggie, let's go inside and see all the delicious-looking pastries!" After they had secured a couple cookies and a cherry Danish each, they left the shop. Both agreed taking a walk around the city center would be a great way to stretch their legs. It was a quaint little town and worthy of a visit. After the car incident, they needed to rest and try to sort out what was happening with the note.

Agnes and Cliff walked to a small well-kept park and sat on a bench to eat their pastries. Suddenly, a medium-sized brown and white terrier mix dog came to their bench. He sat down and eyed the last part of Cliff's cookie. Being a soft touch, Cliff offered it to the waiting canine. The gentle dog took the prized cookie and ate it in one giant gulp.

In the distance someone was calling, "Winston, Winston, where are you?" A nine-year old boy came running up to the rogue dog and snapped a leash on its wiry-haired neck. Agnes asked the cute little boy some questions and if he needed any help with the dog.

"What's your name? I'm guessing the dog's name is Winston."

"I'm Liam. Winston decided to take a walk without me. Thanks for keeping him company until I could get him back on his leash."

Taken in by this small child and amiable animal, Cliff said, "So, is your dog named after Prime Minister Winston Churchill?"

Liam beamed as he answered quickly, "Yes, sir. Mr. Churchill is responsible for keeping Britain safe from Germany and the bombings. It was my dad's idea really. He's in the RAF. Well, we must go now, or my mum will worry about us. See you!" Both boy and dog scrambled across the grass and were soon out of sight.

Cliff and Agnes had a good laugh about the antics of the Irish sounding boy named Liam and his hungry dog Winston. Maybe someday they would have a smart little boy like him, thought Cliff.

"Aggie let's stay all night here and return to High Wycombe tomorrow morning. Sound like a good idea to you?"

"Sure, this looks like a great place to end our wonderful honeymoon."

~~~~~~~~

The Nazis were very disappointed and angry the mission had stalled Once the cook and mechanic were out of the way, he could retrieve the painting from its safe hiding place. The contact had to act now, so they could redeem themselves in the eyes of the Reich.

"I'm being pressured to get the painting to Berlin. You need to take care of the problem at High Wycombe now," she said irritably to the mole.

"This is a military base after all. There are people with guns around all the time."

Trying to flatter him, she replied, "You are a smart guy — figure it out. I'm coming to see you this weekend."

"I will devise a plan to eliminate them from our lives and deliver the goods," he said hoping it would work.

"Contact me when the problem no longer exists. Understand?" the enemy agent said.

"Sure. You are very clear," he replied stiffly, wishing he had never agreed to this impossible plan. She was not the woman he used to know since her return from Germany.

"This will all be over soon." She hung up the phone.

The War Rages On
High Wycombe, England
March 1944

March 15 – March 22, 1944

"The 78th British Division makes headway (in the war) thanks to the support of Allied armor; however, with mounting losses in both manpower and tanks, further Allied thrusts are called off."

Chapter 17

"Aggie, welcome back! Tell me it was wonderful! How was the scenery and the Red Lion Hotel? Did you have a great time on your honeymoon?   Of course, you did…just look at your smiling face!" Emily laughed.

"Sure, Cliff and I had a marvelous time.   I love him so much…I always have! The Red Lion Hotel was perfect, and Clovelly and St. Agnes were lovely beautiful places. We enjoyed the beach and the scenery, plus the wonderful food; however, we did have a few problems during our time away."

"What do you mean, Aggie?   What kind of problems? Are you and Cliff okay?" Emily asked a dozen questions, as Aggie sat down wearily.

Agnes filled in Emily on the ransacked room, the flat tires, and the near hit by the dark blue car on the way to St. Agnes. "I'm sure it all can be explained." Agnes tried to downplay how scared she was during the 'accidents' they had experienced during their honeymoon trip to the coast. She didn't want Emily to worry about Cliff and her even though the speeding car did scare her.

"Aggie, that's terrible. I hope your honeymoon wasn't ruined with all those troubles. I think it's time to tell Lieutenant MacGregor about everything. Even though she frightens me sometimes, she is fair and will help you. Give it some thought, okay?"

Just as they finished their conversation, Sergeant Elderhurst walked in the door of the Mess Hall. "Sergeant Ray, you have been called to the commissary for some explanation of your most recent food orders. I am to bring you over to talk to the officer on duty. Are you ready to go?" he asked. It was more of an order than a suggestion to Agnes.

"Yes, sure. Let me get my hat, and I'll be ready. Emily, go ahead with today's menu, and I will be back as soon as possible. Also, if Cliff comes by please tell him where I have gone. Okay? By the way, do we need anything while I am over there? I'll check the supply room before I go..."

"Sergeant Ray, we need to go now. Would you please come along with me!" interrupted Sergeant Elderhurst irritably. Agnes looked at Emily with a bewildered expression and followed Sergeant Elderhurst to his jeep parked in front of the Mess Hall.

Agnes climbed into the front seat beside him and stared straight ahead. She felt like one of her students who had just been corrected for saying the wrong thing. The jeep pulled away and out the front gate, "Where are we going, Sergeant Elderhurst? The Commissary is not this way. I thought you said the Commissary?"

"Just relax, Sergeant Ray. I am just following orders. *This will all be over soon.*" Sergeant Elderhurst replied sharply and continued to drive onto the road leading away from the base.

"Okay Sergeant, but where are we going?" Agnes replied nervously looking back over her shoulder thinking this didn't seem right.

"You'll find out. Now quit asking so many questions, Sergeant Ray!" As his anger increased so did his speed. The jeep weaved over to the other side of the road then returned to its proper place with a jerk.

"Hey, look where you are going. I want to go back to the base now!" Agnes yelled angrily.

"In the Army, you don't always get what you want, do you?"

Since he was arguing with Agnes, Sergeant Elderhurst didn't notice the black limo advancing behind them. Then came the bump. He thought why are they getting involved in this matter? I'm following orders – just as I was told. The next bump pushed their jeep down the steep incline. Darkness followed both Agnes and Sergeant Elderhurst.

Thinking she had a terrible headache; Agnes opened her eyes and felt her head throb terribly. What's happened? Where is Sergeant Elderhurst?

As she climbed the steep incline, she called, "Sergeant Elderhurst, are you hurt? We should get away from the jeep. It could explode!" There was no answer from Sergeant Elderhurst. Looking down at the still body, she saw blood covering his face. Agnes thought he may have just gotten what he deserved if he was behind the theft of the painting and her kidnapping.

Climbing to the road, she saw a small red car approaching; she waved it down and ran toward the car. "Help, we had an accident, and I think a man is dead down there!" Agnes explained to the woman who had stopped to assist her.

"I'm so sorry for you. Get in the car, and I will take you for help." Agnes hesitated for a few minutes wanting to tell Cliff about the accident and Sergeant Elderhurst. If she left, how could Cliff find her? The kind young woman urged Agnes to get into her car.

Getting in the car, Agnes felt the bump on her head getting larger and hurting more. The young woman asked Agnes, "Are you okay? That's quite a bump on your head."

Touching her pounding head again, she wasn't so sure anymore; however, she responded, "Yes, I think so, but I'm sure I'll be sore tomorrow," thinking she needed to reach the base and tell them what had happened to Sergeant Elderhurst and her. Also, by this time, Cliff would be looking for her.

The young woman's kind voice broke into her thoughts, "What's your name?" she asked as they drove away from the accident scene.

"I'm Sergeant Ray from the base at High Wycombe. Thanks for helping me. I'm feeling a little weak right now." She thought she might pass out, but she needed to stay awake until Cliff found her...

"Sure, you are. *It will all be over soon* so just lean back and relax. My name is Skye Marlowe, and I will take care of you until you feel better."

Skye thought that Mark Elderhurst always messed everything up. Couldn't he carry out his orders! What am I going to do with her now? It's a good thing I was following them too! I wonder why the black limo was trying to get rid of them or just him?"

~~~~~~~~

Back at High Wycombe ~

Coming into the Mess Hall, Cliff asked Emily if she had seen Agnes. "Agnes left with Sergeant Elderhurst about two hours ago. He said she was needed at the commissary. I can't imagine why she would be gone this long, can you?"

Thinking this can't be a good thing, Cliff began to worry. "No, I can't. I think I'll head over there and see what's keeping her. We have plans for this evening. I know she wouldn't be late," Cliff said puzzled as he went out the door. It wasn't like Agnes to be gone this long. Did something happen to her?

Running back to the hangar area, "Hey, Bob, can I borrow that jeep for a while? I need to look for Agnes," Cliff yelled to his good friend, Bob, who was waiting for repairs on his B-25.

"Well, as long as it's not too long, Cliff. You know how the lieutenant is if he has to walk too far! Anyway, I'm waiting on the plane now. Sure, take it away!"

Jumping into the jeep, "thanks!" he yelled on the way over to the commissary to see if Agnes was there. Barely turning off the engine, Cliff leaped out of the driver's seat and headed into the commissary. "Has anyone seen Sergeant Agnes Ray or Sergeant Elderhurst today?"

"Sorry, Sergeant Ray, I haven't seen either one of them today? Of course, I have been really busy...anyone seen Ray or Elderhurst today?" he asked the guys in the back. "Doesn't appear anyone has seen them, sorry!"

"Okay, I'll see if they left the base. Thanks for checking, Corporal." Cliff quickly rushed back to the jeep and started the engine. Where could she be? Why would she be with him? These thoughts rushed through his head, as he gunned the engine and headed to the front gate of the base.

"Has Sergeant Agnes Ray or Sergeant Mark Elderhurst left base today?" Cliff asked the guard on duty tensely.

"I'll check the records for you, Sergeant Ray."

Coming back to the jeep, the guard said, "Yes, it looks like they left about two and half hours ago – about 1500 hours. They didn't have orders, but it seemed okay to let them go."

"Okay, I will be back as soon as I find them. Thanks." Quickly, he headed out the gate before the guard could respond.

Cliff thought, *this is crazy!* Where would they have gone together? I wish there was some way to call her. Luckily, there aren't a lot of roads in this part of England. Looking at the narrow road ahead, he thought, oh, no! I think those are skid marks on the pavement. Cliff stopped the jeep and jumped out to investigate a possible accident scene. Thinking the worst, he started down the deep ravine where he spotted the overturned jeep.

"Oh, please let her be safe!" he said aloud. Carefully, he tried to open the jeep door. Sergeant Elderhurst was obviously dead, but Agnes was not in the jeep. He thought...hopefully, she was not thrown out of the jeep on impact. "Agnes, where are you?" Cliff yelled to an empty hillside. Where is she now?

After searching the area around the jeep, Cliff headed back up the hill to his waiting vehicle. He thought, *what do I do now? How do I find her without Sergeant Elderhurst to question?*

He thought, I'll try searching for her further down the road on the other side of the hill. If I don't find her, I'll head back to the base and report the accident to the guard on duty. *Where could Agnes be?*

~~~~~~~~

Skye helped Agnes into the sparely furnished room and guided her to a chair near the window. "Would you like to have a cup of hot tea? You look a little pale after going down the hill back there. Also, there is blood on your arm. I'll bring a bandage and some tea while you rest."

Agnes thought it was truly a blessing this nice woman was there to help. "Thanks so much. I appreciate your kindness, but I should let the base know where I am. Also, Sergeant Elderhurst will have to be identified and brought back to the base...but, I think I will shut my eyes for just a minute," Agnes said, more shook up than she thought. The pain in her arm was starting to get worse as her head continued to ache.

Skye always traveled with a small first aid kit. She took what she needed from the kit and looked for the rope she had brought in from her car. Skye gathered the bandages, made the tea, and brought the rope into the room where Agnes had fallen asleep. She hid the rope behind the sofa, as Agnes opened her eyes and took the tea from Skye. "Thanks so much." Agnes saw the rope that Skye hid behind the sofa. *I wonder what she is going to do with that rope.*

"After I get your arm bandaged, we will notify the base. Right now, just relax. *This will all be over soon*," Skye said sympathetically.

Agnes closed her eyes and thought, that was a strange thing to say, '*This will all be over soon*'-- I think that was exactly what Sergeant Elderhurst said to me when he picked me up at the Mess Hall. Maybe this young woman isn't who she appears to be. Agnes thought she better come up with a plan quickly if she were going to leave here alive.

Skye cleaned the blood off Agnes' arm and put a bandage over the small nasty puncture wound Agnes received during the accident. She wanted to gain Agnes' trust before she shut her up for good. Skye gathered all the leftover bandages and took them to the kitchen. Since Agnes looked drowsy, it would soon be time to put her plan into action.

Agnes pretended to be asleep as her enemy approached. Even in her weakened position, when Skye came near to her with the rope, Agnes overpowered Skye and tied her to a kitchen chair. After Skye was rendered harmless, Agnes mused, *I guess my basic training and marching strengthened my muscles.* "You were no match for me, Skye. So, start talking...what are you up to? Do you know Mark Elderhurst?"

Skye replied angrily, "I'm not talking to you! This is all your fault! If you and your boyfriend had stayed out of our business, none of this would have happened! Let me go!"

"I don't think you are going anywhere for a while. Our country doesn't like your kind. I have a feeling you're working for the Nazis." Agnes thought, *things are beginning to make sense to me now. I need to get some help and get word to Cliff about where I am.* "So, Skye, just relax, *this will all be over soon!* I think that's a phrase you will understand!" Agnes said with pleasure.

Agnes left Skye tied up and ran to the road hoping to flag down someone to help. After about fifteen minutes, she spotted a U.S. Army jeep coming down the road. Fortunately, Cliff saw Agnes standing on the side of road and pulled to a stop right in front of her, "Hey, Cliff, you always know when I need you, don't you! Come and meet someone who has been giving us some trouble for some time!"

Cliff climbed out of the jeep, hugged Aggie gently as he said, "How are you, Aggie? I saw the overturned jeep. Your arm is bandaged...were you in the jeep with Elderhurst? What are you talking about?"

Agnes laughed, "Now, you are getting carried away and asking all these questions at once! Yes, I am okay except for a bump on the head and a wound on my arm. Skye bandaged it before she tried to tie me up! Come on, follow me, and I will explain what I know about our mystery. Then we need to go for help and take Skye back to the base for questioning. She has a lot of explaining to do about the Escape Kit and the missing painting from Harlaxton Manor."

Cliff put his arm around Agnes and gave her another quick hug. "I am so glad I found you. When I saw that Elderhurst was dead, I didn't know what had happened to you. Okay, let's get this mystery woman secured in the jeep for interrogation back at the base. Good work, Red!" Cliff and Agnes put an angry Skye Marlowe into the jeep and prepared to return to High Wycombe.

Cliff gingerly helped Agnes into the front seat of the jeep and started the engine. "Are you sure you are okay, Aggie? That was quite a trip down the ravine back there."

"I'm feeling a little sore, but I don't think there is anything permanently damaged! I'm eager to get Skye Marlowe back to base right now and tell Emily, Midge, and Ruth what just happened. I know Ruth will be concerned I haven't come back. Did you talk to her, Cliff?"

"Yes, you're right. I did talk to her – that's how I knew you were missing – and with whom. That's when I thought I needed to start looking for you. It didn't make sense that Elderhurst needed to take you anywhere off base," Cliff explained on the short ride back to base.

The Mystery Couple are Revealed
High Wycombe, England
April 1944

"Two main organizations were responsible for intelligence activities in World War II for the Allies. These were the British SOE, or Special Operations Executive, and the American OSS, or Office of Strategic Services."

Chapter 18

Pulling up to the administration office's entrance, Cliff and Agnes took Skye into the general's office to explain what they knew about her and Elderhurst. They needed to lay out everything they knew about the coded message on the note, the Escape Kit that was dropped with their gear, the missing expensive smoked damaged painting from Harlaxton, the threatening notes, and nearly being run over by a speeding car. It would make more sense if they explained all these events. "I'm sure Intelligence will be interested in our story," Cliff said patiently to Agnes.

"Cliff, Elderhurst was just trying to keep an eye on us all the time we were at Harlaxton. It wasn't a coincidence he was our driver and found us at that pub in London. He must have been following us all the time. I wonder how he and Skye are connected?"

The diligent pair of sleuths wondered who Elderhurst and Skye Marlowe were working for? The Nazis? Then Agnes told Cliff where they had seen Skye before today. "You know what? We have seen Skye before today! Do you remember when we went to *The Gregory* for some hot tea and dessert? Well, she was the barmaid! She looks so different now – she cut her hair and dyed it black! I figured it out when I was at her house after the accident. Okay – now…I have more questions than answers again! Here comes the corporal, I think we are about to be asked numerous questions ourselves like…why didn't you come forward before this got out of hand?"

"Corporal, we have to talk with the general immediately. I'm Sergeant Cliff Ray and this is Sergeant Agnes Ray. We have some information and someone I think the general will be interested in meeting." Cliff informed the corporal briefly. The corporal left Cliff and Agnes and went to tell the general's assistant their story.

When the general's assistant came out to the large, vaulted and marble-floored lobby, he said, "Why is the young lady tied up, Sergeant Ray? I hope you have a good reason for interrupting the general today," he said roughly.

Organizing their story in his head, he stated, "Yes, I think we have a very good reason for bringing her to the general. Can we go in now?" Pushing Skye toward General Sullivan's office.

"Yes, follow me." The irritated corporal led the trio down the hall and into the general's office.

"Okay, Sergeant Ray, what's this all about? It better be important or you may be spending some time in the brig yourself," General Sullivan's growled.

Starting at the beginning of this saga, Cliff began telling their story to the general. "Sergeant Ray and I were sent to Harlaxton Manor to deliver a message to RAF General Stevens a few months ago. While we were there a valuable painting was stolen from Harlaxton Manor. I think we found part of the team here. Her accomplice appears to be Sergeant Mark Elderhurst whom I found dead after a jeep accident. He kidnapped Sergeant Ray. After he was killed in the accident, she was taken by Skye Marlowe to a house nearby. Sergeant Ray was able to overpower her and tie her up," Cliff explained to the general.

The general looked over at Skye Marlowe and Agnes. "Good work, Sergeant Ray, okay, go on. I am interested in the rest of the story. Why did they want a painting from Harlaxton? How is Sergeant Elderhurst involved?" General Sullivan quizzed Cliff and Agnes.

Agnes began where Cliff left off, "Sergeant Elderhurst was our driver to Harlaxton. We think he followed us while we were in London and tried to run us over when we were in Clovelly on our honeymoon."

General Sullivan interrupted Agnes, "Congratulations, by the way, but how are the two of them connected? What were they going to do with a valuable painting?"

"Perhaps, I should go back to the beginning, and then I think you will want to ask Miss Marlowe some questions too. When I first arrived at High Wycombe, someone dropped an Escape Kit with my gear. No one came to claim it, but it's not something that is just lying around. I hid it in a safe place, but later a secret message was given to me by a woman aviator, Ella Cook. She found it on her plane when she arrived here. The note mentioned a castle near Grantham and a mission. We didn't understand all of it, but maybe Skye could fill you in with what we don't know."

Agnes glanced though the window of the general's office door where Skye was being guarded by the corporal on duty. Skye's face looked like stone as she stared at the floor. Agnes hoped Skye got what she deserved for her traitorous actions.

General Sullivan thought over what he had just heard. There was some talk among his staff about a mole in the ranks. Intelligence had been following up on some leads and messages they had intercepted a few days ago. Perhaps these two events were connected. He would have to bring Colonel Mills into this conversation.

"Okay, I guess we are ready to call in Colonel Mills, head of Military Intelligence, to do some interrogation of Miss Marlowe. Thanks, Sergeant Ray and Sergeant Ray, but we will take it from here. I am sure Colonel Mills will want to talk to you both some more, plus collect the note and the Escape Kit that you have safely tucked away. You two are dismissed and thanks for your help," Sullivan said.

Two days later ~

A jeep pulled up to the door of the Mess Hall. Cliff was sitting in the front seat. The driver came to the door and asked for Agnes. "Colonel Mills, Military Intelligence

Office would like to speak with you Sergeant Ray. You may want to put someone in charge while you are gone. It could be some time before you return, Sergeant."

Agnes thought of the last jeep ride. That was almost her 'last' ride. Looking around at the girls, she muttered, "Oh, sure. Uh...Ruth, would you and Emily take charge of lunch. I will be back as soon as I can."

Emily, always eager to help her friend, quickly added, "Aggie, don't worry about things here. The menu is already prepared, and Ruth and I know the routine."

Walking to the jeep, Agnes was surprised to see Cliff. "Hi, Cliff. I guess we find out some answers to our mysteries today! Maybe we can finally relax without someone looking over our shoulders or following us!" Cliff smiled at Agnes and gave her a wink. Agnes smiled and climbed into the back seat of the jeep. She sure loved this man!

After arriving at headquarters, Cliff helped Agnes out of the backseat and followed her inside. Upon entering the area near Colonel Mills' office, they were told to have a seat and wait until called. "There is always a lot of waiting in the Army. Have you noticed that Cliff?"

Cliff said finally, "I'm just hoping the colonel likes our answers, and we discover what was up with Elderhurst and Skye Marlowe."

Agnes thought, I'm sure we will be asked plenty of questions about what we know and when we knew it. "I hope I don't lose my sergeant's stripes! I wouldn't like to peel potatoes for the rest of my enlistment. What would my family think of us?"

As usual, Cliff was trying to make her feel better when he said, "Ah, Aggie, you are such a good cook they wouldn't do that to you...now, maybe the Army would do that to me though!"

Aggie sat thinking this building was once a school and how different it was now with all the military people walking about. She imagined young eager students walking these halls instead of soldiers. Looking down the hallway, now referred to as the "war room" where the war briefings were held, she saw generals with several stars on their uniforms walking in their direction. What was next for them if things didn't go well?

While they were waiting in the lobby, the door to the war room opened and shut several times as the general's staff, and other important visitors, were being briefed on the war news. Aggie looked at Cliff and said, "I hope the war is going our way now. This war has been going on for way too long. I know that you haven't been back home since November 1941, before the war started. There are many other soldiers like you too."

Finally, the door opened, and Colonel Mills asked them to come into his office and have a seat. "Well, Sgts. Ray and Ray, you've had quite an adventure, haven't you? I have some questions for you and a few answers!"

"First of all, how did you get the note you decoded? Didn't you think you should have turned it over to headquarters instead of trying to solve this case yourself?"

Agnes swallowed suddenly and her mind went blank. She thought she should tell the colonel everything she knew. "Well, sir, I made a promise to Ella Cook I wouldn't tell anyone but Cliff about the note. Then, Corporal Emily Smith and I found the Escape Kit in our gear. I tried to tell my superior officer about it, but she ushered us off to the Mess Hall. Then, all these events seemed to be related to the note. After we went to Harlaxton, lots of things happened, and it was important to us to see it through to the end. We never suspected Sergeant Elderhurst of being involved in this plot or whatever he was doing. Then Skye Marlowe found me after the crash. That's when I recognized her as the barmaid from *The Gregory*, a pub near Harlaxton."

Cliff had been sitting quietly as Agnes told the story and how all the events of the past couple of months had unfolded. He had been wondering about the black limo for some time and thought he should ask about it. Before he could open his mouth, Agnes said, "Colonel Mills, there is something that I don't understand. Why was a black limo following the jeep? I looked back once I realized that Sergeant Elderhurst was up to no good, and I saw a black limo following us," Agnes asked.

Undoubtedly, Agnes and Cliff thought they were serving their country by tenaciously trying to solve the mystery. After the couple explained their actions to Colonel Mills, he began to soften his attitude toward them.

"Sergeant Ray, I am not at liberty to tell you anything about the black limo or what we know about Elderhurst's activities. Let's just say he was under investigation – which I'm sure you have already figured out being such good detectives," Colonel Mills smiled slowly.

Agnes blushed and looked for support from Cliff across the room, "Certainly, I understand sir. What else do you want to know?" Agnes asked politely.

"There was a gardener at Harlaxton who was involved with Skye Marlowe. Actually, Skye Marlowe is Sam's daughter. We believe she was forcing him to give her information about some of the RAF's operations at Harlaxton. Her parents have been under surveillance for some time, and we are searching for them now. They are involved in this plot to some degree. Again, I can only tell you a limited amount concerning this situation. We presume she was forcing them to help her and Sergeant Elderhurst steal the painting."

Taking in all this new information, Cliff outlined what they knew about Sam and Sarah Marlowe. "Well, we found Sam in the garden and someone had hit him on the head. He didn't want to report the incident to anyone at Harlaxton. When we went back to check on him, he and his wife were gone. So, now it makes sense that he wouldn't want anyone to know about his connection to Skye and Elderhurst."

"We are also looking for the painting Elderhurst stole from Harlaxton. We think that he wanted to sell the painting and send the money to Berlin. He was supposed to get it to Switzerland by March 5th. Someone was going to pick it up and make the arrangements for a sale there. The painting also contained some numbers which could give the Nazis information about an upcoming major campaign being planned by our top generals. This is a serious breach of security, and we must get the painting back for several reasons. Where do you think it could be?" Colonel Mills asked Cliff and Agnes.

Looking at each other, Cliff and Agnes decided to divulge what their search of the tunnels had uncovered. Pulling the pieces of paper from his pocket, Cliff explained, "Well, one thing we found in the coal tunnel at Harlaxton was this note. I don't know if its related to this case of not, but here it is." Cliff handed over the pieces of paper to the colonel.

Cliff continued his account of their visit to Harlaxton, "Agnes and I arranged the torn pieces of paper to try to decipher the words written on the paper. It appears to be a note from Skye to Elderhurst.

"Apparently, she was desperate to get the painting out of Harlaxton by March 5th," Agnes added.

"Where do you think the painting could be hidden at Harlaxton, Sergeant Ray? I assume you and Sergeant Ray looked several places at the manor for the painting. Where would you hide it if you were trying to stash an expensive picture?" Colonel Mills asked the pair.

"Well, there are at least four more tunnels we didn't check because we were called back to High Wycombe. There are numerous large fireplaces and nooks and crannies in the manor. Let me think a little while about where the logical place might be," Cliff remarked.

Agnes thought a few minutes and wasn't sure she should share her thoughts with the men. They might think she was just being silly. Well, she might as well tell them what she was thinking. Plunging right into the conversation, she said knowingly, "I realize this isn't logical, but I would hide it in the kitchen! It's a place that no one else would think to look and easy to get to. No one would suspect you were up to anything illegal."

The men looked at Agnes curiously, "Okay, Agnes, sometimes women think about things in a different way. Where would you hide it in the kitchen?" Colonel Mills inquired of Agnes.

Not sure whether or not to be insulted with his comment, she continued with her answer, "Well, I would place it inside a large pot high on a shelf which was not easily accessible. At Harlaxton, there are plenty of odd little nooks and shelves. Thanks for not laughing at me."

Cliff was proud of Aggie for not being intimidated by the colonel. She had a sharp mind and was the smartest women he knew. Of course, his view of women might be a bit slanted toward this particular woman. "Hey, Aggie, I think you are the best crime fighter in the Army. Of course, I am prejudiced, I guess," Cliff remarked quietly as Colonel Mills made some notes about their questioning session.

"Sir, I am still not clear about why that particular painting would be worth all this trouble. Yes, it was valuable because it is one of the only items still connected to the Gregory family, but is that enough money to risk being killed or court martialed?" Cliff asked of the colonel.

"Well, I guess you two deserve some answers, but this information cannot leave this room. There is a code written in the picture. It has to do with the number of fence posts in the front of the picture. I can't reveal any more information, but also its priceless to the Harlaxton owner, Violet Van der Elst, and she would pay a hundred thousand pounds or more to get it back. As though, that isn't enough, there was another old painting underneath it, Blue Boy by Gainsborough. It is extremely valuable as you can imagine."

"Okay, I understand the money and what that would mean to the Nazis as this war drags on, but who was paying Sergeant Elderhurst? How did Skye Marlowe and her parents get involved in all this mess?" Agnes asked patiently.

"From our interrogation sessions with Ms. Marlowe, we discovered she is a foreign agent for Germany. The Germans contacted her to get the painting for them. She was dating Sergeant Elderhurst and convinced him to help her. She worked at the pub near Harlaxton, The Gregory."

What makes someone turn against their country? Is money that important for happiness? Goodness knows, my family has been without much money, and we are certainly happy, Agnes thought to herself.

"It is somewhat public knowledge Sergeant Elderhurst was a well-known ladies' man. He was billeted at the major's home. Gossip has it Elderhurst became too friendly with the major's wife. So, his death is under investigation for that reason as well. Since Sam and Sarah Marlowe have disappeared, we haven't been able to question them about their part in all this yet," Colonel Mills explained.

Standing up and walking over to the window Colonel Mills seemed to be pondering whether to tell the Rays anymore about the situation. He didn't want to interfere with the investigation. There were still so many unknowns in this case, he thought.

"I will send a team to Harlaxton to check the kitchen. Do you have any other questions?" Colonel Mills asked Agnes and Cliff.

"What will happen to Skye Marlowe?" Agnes asked.

Colonel Mills liked this couple and wanted to answer all their questions, but some questions would have to remain unanswered. They were sharp young people and maybe they could figure it out themselves.

"I'm not at liberty to answer, Agnes," as he winked at her secretly. Agnes smiled, interpreting his unspoken answer, and rose to leave with Cliff.

"Again, thanks for all your help with this investigation. Agnes, I hope you weren't hurt seriously in the crash with Elderhurst."

Unconsciously touching her bruised head, Agnes replied, "No, I'm a bit sore even now, but I'm sure I'll recover."

"Oh, I forgot to ask. How did the note get into Ella Cook's plane?" Cliff asked the colonel.

Even though all the facts weren't confirmed positively, Colonel Mills could say with some confidence, "Skye Marlowe was one of the women pilots who came with Jacqueline Cochran's group. Somehow, she slipped through our check points. She was a very clever agent who knew how to evade our procedures. After arriving here from the United States, she got a job at *The Gregory*. She knew her parents lived on the grounds of Harlaxton, and she could coerce them into helping her with her mission. I'm certainly glad she is in custody now thanks to you two. Good job!"

"It was our pleasure, Colonel."

Saluting Colonel Mills' Cliff and Agnes left his office and headed back to the Mess Hall for a cup of coffee. Cliff thought I'm delighted that Skye Marlowe is no longer working for the Nazis. It's just very disturbing that someone like her can cause such damage to our country. I hope her parents are okay and far away from danger.

Agnes silently thought how pleased she was they were able to do their part in taking Skye Marlowe and Mark Elderhurst out of the spy system in Britain. How could they betray their country?

As Agnes turned her attention back to Cliff, he remarked, "Elderhurst is what we would call a rascal in Tennessee. He's probably the person who hit Sam Marlowe on the head. Sam was probably arguing with Elderhurst or unwilling to cooperate. I guess we will never know exactly what happened to them."

Agnes lovingly laid her hand on Cliff's arm and quietly replied, "Hey, we didn't find out how the Escape Kit is connected to the rest of the mystery. I don't think Colonel Mills would be open to answering anymore of our questions right now. Perhaps, we'll have to figure it out ourselves."

The pair tried to map out the following information. The Escape Kit is the only thing they hadn't figured out yet. Cliff pondered how the kit got mixed in with Agnes' gear. They would have to think about some possible ideas of how everything and everyone was connected to each other.

1. They are given to soldiers that are going into potential danger.

2. They are packed with items that could be traded with the enemy or friendly civilians for information.

3. What is in this Escape Kit?

4. How did it get mixed in with Agnes' gear without her or Emily seeing who dropped it?

5. What do we do with it now?

After looking over the information Cliff had written on the paper, she said, "What's your opinion about the black limo, Cliff? Do you think it's tied to the Escape Kit or another person altogether? Could it have been Sergeant Elderhurst's kit?"

Giving it some thought, Cliff replied, "That's still difficult to determine. Aggie, where is the Escape Kit now? I would like to take a look at it. Maybe there's a clue in it or the items will help us to figure this out. Where do we go now?"

Trying to hide her amusement, she replied, "Cliff, think a minute here. Where would a cook hide something, she didn't want anyone else to find?" Agnes teased Cliff with a knowing smile on her face.

"In the kitchen, of course!"

"You are such a smart man and a good listener too!"

Agnes thought, not many people go traipsing through my kitchen, and the girls who work there pretty much just follow orders. So, they left to see if the kit was still there. Agnes hurried Cliff along to the Mess Hall and into the clean gleaming kitchen. Agnes took pride in keeping her work area sparkling clean and up to Army regs.

"Okay, Cliff, get a chair and lift the huge soup kettle down from the top shelf. I think you will find the Escape Kit inside unless someone else has guessed where I hide things!"

Easing the tall stainless-steel soup kettle down from the top shelf, Agnes opened the lid. "Here it is, Cliff, just the way I left it a few months ago. Let's look at the items inside. I don't see anyone else around, so this would be good time to look it over."

Opening the Escape Kit and laying the items out on the counter. Agnes thought, this is the last of the mysteries to be solved. Cliff studied the items for a few minutes before saying, "Aggie, this one has some gold in it. I heard there was always some valuable items like a gold necklace or a few ounces of gold. It depends on the area of the world where the soldier in question is located. I think Escape Kits were given primarily to aviators who might be shot down and need these types of items in enemy territory. I would think this kit is for someone in Europe. Let's see what else is in the kit."

Looking over the items, they discovered: a map, some money in British pounds and French marcs, a miniature compass which fits inside a round tin box of powdered toothpaste, some gauze and a tube of ointment, matches, fishing line, knife, some photo paper for forgery purposes and a tiny container of gold nuggets. Who would leave all these things behind? Did they want to hide it on purpose or was it dropped without the owner's knowledge? Would they ever find the answer?

Agnes asked Cliff if he had any ideas about who the owner might be. "Well, from what you have said, and the items contained in the kit, I am thinking it belongs to a pilot or navigator perhaps. Maybe someone who flew in here and wanted to get rid of this kit before it was detected? Seems to make sense to me, but that doesn't give us our answer does it." Agnes studied the items again looking for clues to the ownership of the kit.

Cliff thought this could be one of the pilots I know. Maybe it is a pilot who just stopped by for refueling and dropped it accidentally. Maybe we are making too much out of this one item. "What is your theory?" Agnes inquired of Cliff as she stepped back from the items, but still looking them over for more information.

"So, Aggie, you think that the Escape Kit is not connected to Elderhurst and Sky Marlowe?" Cliff asked puzzled.

"Well, I think that it's a possibility, Cliff." Agnes thought I just can't get it to add up with those two. What reason would they have to need something like this? Other than the possible monetary value of the gold, why would they want it?

"Well, you can't put it on the lost and found bulletin board – 'Has anyone lost an Escape Kit?' or ask people if they want it back? I do like your thought it could be an aviator – well, not really like it, because it would mean it's one of our guys – maybe, even someone I know. I will look around the hangar and maybe make some subtle remarks about who would have a kit and see what happens."

"Sounds like a plan. I think I would like to talk to Ella again to see if she knows anything about it or if there is someone she would suspect. Can't hurt to ask, I guess."

As much as she would have liked to keep discussing the 'what ifs' of this mystery the girls would be here soon for meal preparations. "Make sure you get a break soon. I am trying out a new recipe today!"

Yum!" Cliff said then made a funny face.

Agnes laughed and said, "Hey, I thought you liked my cooking!"

"I do, I do...I was just remembering the last time you tried a new recipe, and we had to eat the fudge with a spoon; but it did taste good, Aggie. Well, I'll see you later." Cliff trotted off before he got into any more trouble with Agnes.

"Okay, see you later, troublemaker!" Agnes yelled after Cliff. Agnes hurried over to the Mess Hall to check on the girls before time to serve again. As she walked into the kitchen, she heard this song,

The K.P.s are Scrubbing Away

Over sinks, over pails

With the Sergeant on our tails

All the K.P.s are scrubbing away

Shining pots, shining pans

Cleaning out garbage cans

All the K.P.s are scrubbing away

Oh, it's Hi! Hi! Hee! In the Kitchen scullery

Sixteen long hours of the day

And Wher'er we go,

By the smell you'll always know,

That the K.P.s are scrubbing away

(Keep em scrubbing)

That the K.P.s are scrubbing away

As Agnes entered the kitchen, she saw Emily, Ruth, and Midge singing and laughing together. They didn't hear the door open, but all the singing stopped when they saw Agnes standing in the doorway with her hands on her hips,

"Well, it looks like the mice will play when the cat's away! So, that's what you think of me, huh?"

The girls looked sheepishly at Agnes and bowed their heads. "Well, Agnes, we just were having some fun...you know how I like a good time. I'm always getting into trouble." Emily replied apologetically.

Agnes started laughing and couldn't stop. With happy tears running down her face she said, "You girls are so funny! I'm not mad...that's a crazy song! Where did you learn that one? We should sing it more often...make it more fun around here. It's been pretty sad since Frankie left," Agnes remarked.

Agnes pulled a letter out of her pocket and shared the latest news with the girls. "Oh, Emily, I got a letter from Vera Slaton today – and now it's Nuckols!" Agnes filled in Midge and Ruth that Vera was one of their friends from basic training in Florida. "Yes, she married her boyfriend Chester in May. I know they will be happy for a long time!"

Emily replied, "Hey, that's great! I'm so happy for her!" She thought, gosh, I wish we could have gone to the wedding. Maybe we can get together, when the war is over and celebrate. War is very tough on relationships, but Cliff and Agnes discovered how much they mean to each other. It appears that Vera and Chester have also!

The Invasion

High Wycombe, England

June 6, 1944

The D-Day invasion was one of the most important battles fought during WWII. It involved all branches of the military and Allied forces. General Eisenhower and his advisors were gauging the weather and trying to launch a surprise attack against the Germans. Allied forces would cross the English Channel and begin their attack on the dangerous beaches of Normandy.

Chapter 19

The D-day invasion which took place June 6, 1944 was the largest amphibious invasion in history and changed the course of the war. Nearly 200,000 Allied troops boarded ships and more than 3,000 aircraft headed toward Normandy.

"Aggie, have you heard the scuttlebutt? There's a big offensive planned for today. The base is on high alert and the planes must be inspected and all the pilots are getting their gear together. I can't stay long, but I wanted to talk to you about this bit of news." Cliff poured himself a cup of coffee and sat down at a nearby table.

"I'm sorry all the guys are in danger again. That's what the buzz has been the last few days around here. I'm just praying that the causalities will be light, and all our guys will come back safely. This war has been going on too long especially for the British," Agnes lamented looking over at Cliff.

"Yes, I agree. I have become good friends with many of the pilots and navigators and wouldn't like to see anything happen to any of them --- I know it's war and it's not good to get too close to anybody – well, except you Aggie!"

Agnes gave Cliff a sad smile and quizzed him about what he knew about the upcoming big plans. "Have you heard any of the details about when the attack started and where our soldiers are headed?"

"Well, not exactly because I'm sure the top brass would want to keep that information top secret, but I did overhead some of the pilots say they weren't leaving from Calais, the shortest route in the channel to France, as the Germans thought. We certainly want to surprise the Germans and retake Paris. The French have suffered enough, as have all the European countries under Nazi control. Aggie, we're lucky we were born in America."

"Sure thing, Cliff. Here comes Ruth with some questions about lunch, so I'll see you after dinner. Let me know if you hear anything else about the invasion. I'll be thinking about all our fly guys and the British RAF pilots too," Agnes replied sadly.

Today would be a difficult day until they heard what was happening over the channel. It was challenging to keep her mind on cooking. How many men and planes would the Allies lose during this huge invasion?

Agnes walked back with Ruth to the kitchen to answer her question about the supply of green beans delivered from a local farmer. "Agnes, what do you think about these green beans? They look a little pale to me. Do you think they will be okay to serve?"

Looking over the pile of beans, Agnes thought stewing over pale green beans wasn't too important right now. "Well, they aren't the great beans that my dad grows in Tennessee, but they look like they will do for today's meal." Tears starting to fall, she began to break up the beans and put them in the large cooking pans.

"Agnes, what's wrong?"

Agnes replied, "Ruth, I am just so tired of the killing and the war. I wish it would be over today, and Cliff and I could go home. I want to go to college at Middle Tennessee State College to be a teacher. I think Cliff would like to do that too."

I'm sure the invasion is already happening. I'm just sad there's going to be lots of deaths. Maybe, even some of the guys that come in here to eat in our Mess Hall. They will pay with their lives, so all the folks at home can live freely. It's a lot to think about – that's all. Well, that's enough tears for today – I will get the beans cleaned and cooked. There are hungry soldiers to feed! Agnes dried her tears and got started on the green beans.

After dinner ~

Agnes saw Cliff standing in the field staring at the sky; when she approached him, she said, "Cliff, I haven't seen you all day. Aren't you hungry or are you avoiding me?"

Turning to Agnes, he replied, "I will come by for a few minutes to see you and get something quick to eat. You know me...I can't get enough to eat. Of course, I'm not mad at you silly!" Cliff reached out and pulled Aggie close to him for a brief hug. She was glad he was on the ground and not up in a plane.

Turning his gaze back to the sky, he remembered how some of the planes had not returned at all. Some of his friends had gone down in the ocean or worse in the hands of the enemy. One day last week there was a bomber with a damaged landing gear that had crashed and burst into flames on the landing strip. It was something that you couldn't get out of your mind. It was hard to talk about too, even to Aggie.

Finally, he said, "Some of my pilots have returned with smoke coming out the tail of their plane – just barely making it back here before they crashed. As you know, it may take six or eight hours before we know how many have made it back." It was impossible to work on these planes and talk to the pilots without worrying about their safety. They are putting it all on the line going up in these treacherous skies.

"Aggie, the planes have been coming back from France with bullet holes or worse all day. I've got to get them repaired, so they can go back out as quickly as possible. As usual, we don't have enough supplies or help to do all we need to do today."

"Oh sure, Cliff. I know that some of these pilots are your friends, and you are worried about their safety – not just the plane. I'll be back in a flash with a sandwich for you.

How about the other guys? Do you want me to send some cookies back to you or a stack of sandwiches?"

"Aggie, I'll go with you to the Mess Hall and bring the food back here for the guys and me. I need a break for a few minutes." Walking back to the Mess Hall, Agnes rushed to the kitchen to make some ham sandwiches and pack up some peanut butter cookies. The girls liked to have some extra treats on hand in case the guys showed up and were hungry. They couldn't turn them away without something to eat.

A few minutes later, she appeared in the room and found Cliff asleep with his head on his arm. She hated to wake him knowing that he had put in some very long days and nights recently; however, if he didn't get back to repairing some of these bombers soon... "Cliff, I have your sandwiches now. You better head back to the hangar before someone comes looking for you. Hope you get some sleep soon! I'm afraid for our soldiers today. Have you heard any news yet?" Agnes asked in a concerned voice.

Snapping awake and rubbing his eyes, he remarked, "I'm afraid not, Aggie. See you tomorrow. Take care, love." Grabbing the bags of sandwiches and cookies, Cliff turned and started toward the door just as Cliff's friend Bob walked into the Mess Hall. "Hi, Cliff. I needed a break from all the action."

Cliff grinned at Agnes before getting up to leave for the hangars. "I better get these sandwiches and cookies back to the guys before they send out a search party or think I've gone AWOL."

Cliff gave Bob a wave and headed back to work. Bob smiled at Agnes and found a seat, "Where's the coffee? I'm all keyed up with the invasion chatter going around. Also, would there be any of that special chocolate cake you made left over from lunch, Agnes?"

"Sure, Bob. I'll see what I can find in the kitchen."

Agnes wondered what Bob knew about the invasion. "Hey, Bob, what have you heard about the battle now?"

"Cliff has been repairing planes and patching up bullet holes all day. I hope our guys are winning, and I know we have a lot of crack pilots. They are the best! We have been waiting a long time for the day to give it back to the Germans," Bob remarked proudly.

The last report that came in was the Allies had landed on Utah, Gold, and Omaha beaches. There were heavy causalities, but the Allies were holding their own so far. There were planes helping our troops, and the Navy had ships all over the channel. After Bob's plane was repaired, he was taking off. This was one of the biggest offensives which had taken place for some time.

Agnes returned with a big piece of chocolate cake for Bob. "Gee, Agnes, that looks swell. I appreciate it so much. You gals really keep us fed well. Don't think we don't notice all the small special things you do for the guys...not, just Cliff!"

Bob took a drink of the hot coffee and started on his large piece of chocolate cake. "Agnes, how's Cliff holding up with all the damaged planes coming in here day and night? He sure looks tired!"

"I know. Cliff and the other mechanics have been working like the devil trying to keep you fly boys in the air. Sadly, some of the pilots haven't come back. It's very hard on Cliff and the other guys. You know, they get very close to each other. I hope everything is going our way at Normandy. The French people have been suffering for some time as well as the other European countries under Nazi control. Go get 'em, Bob!" Agnes replied sadly.

Agnes sat down across from Bob and asked, "Bob, how are you doing? Everyone looks exhausted all the time these days."

"Well, I have to be honest – I'm ready to go home. I'm torn about it too. I know the Army needs veteran pilots and gunners, but I'm not sure I can be any good to anyone if I don't get away from here for a while. You know, the stress gets to you..."

Finishing his strong black coffee and chocolate cake, Bob started to leave the Mess Hall, but before he left, he turned back and remarked, "Agnes, thanks. I really needed someone to talk to today. I have flown nearly thirty missions over Germany and France. Sometimes, it makes you think about when your number might be up. You know what I mean? I will be eligible to go home soon. I'll miss Cliff a lot. You take care of yourself and that husband of yours!"

"Always, and you do the same, Bob." Agnes gave Bob a smile and a wave goodbye. It was tough saying goodbye to some of the guys – not knowing if you would ever see them again. They are truly American heroes of this war.

~~~~~~~~

Edie had worked through lunch time and was very hungry as she made her way to the Mess Hall. The days had been very difficult for everyone. As she sat down by herself, she had a habit of scanning the room for Aggie when she was eating alone, which was most of the time. She was hoping Aggie had a few minutes to chat with her over a cup of coffee. Aggie was sure to save her a piece of apple pie. Apple was Edie's favorite pie and sometimes it was gone before Edie stopped to eat. Over the last few months, Edie had shared that she was the second oldest in her family and was Valedictorian of her high school class. They seemed to have a lot in common. Their hometowns were just a few miles apart. Maybe they would be friends after the war was over too.

Finally, Aggie finished restocking the shelves and spotted Edie sitting by herself. She grabbed the apple pie she had saved and started toward her table.

"Hey, friend, how's it going today?" Aggie smiled warmly at Edie. Seeing the apple pie in Aggie's hand, she replied, "It just got a whole lot better! Thank you, Aggie. You're a lifesaver!"

Grateful to see Edie smile, Aggie said, "Always delighted to help a fellow Southerner make it through the night." Edie dug into the luscious looking pie.

Aggie suddenly said, "Why are you here for dinner, Edie? You usually come for lunch."

Swallowing the pie carefully she replied slowly, "I'm usually working and don't want to quit what I'm working on to eat."

Thinking it over and wondering why Edie always seemed secretive and guarded about her job, Aggie thought she would just come out and ask her what she did for the military. "Golly, that's devotion for sure. What do you do exactly?" Agnes inquired.

Edie froze mid-bite and wondered how she was going to phrase her answers without giving too much information about her work. She smiled and started to answer Aggie's question when Cliff approached the table.

"Hi girls! That apple pie looks wonderful, Aggie. I hope there's another piece for me in the kitchen." Aggie smiled and said, "I thought you would be full after all that chocolate cake you ate earlier today. I think I can find another piece of apple pie."

Edie saw her way to escape without answering Aggie's question. She said her goodbyes, scooted off her chair, and headed for the door. Deciphering codes had helped many generals know where to place their men during combat. She only hoped her code breaking training was helpful to the invasion today.

~~~~~~~~

As Emily was wiping off tables, she thought it had been a very emotional day for everyone. When she looked up, she saw Lieutenant MacGregor walking toward her. Oh no, what's wrong now!

"Hello, Private Smith. I'm happy you haven't been in my office recently. Is Sergeant Ray here now?"

"I'm happy I haven't been in your office too. I really don't look for trouble – it just finds me! Yes, she's in the kitchen. I'll go get Sergeant Ray; she's never in trouble."

After Emily went to get Aggie, Lieutenant MacGregor smiled at Emily's remark. She thought, some people seemed to attract trouble, and Private Smith seemed to be one of those people. She was a pleasant spirited girl and would eventually come around to the Army way of doing things.

"Lieutenant MacGregor, did you want to see me?" Agnes asked her superior. Lieutenant MacGregor always made her nervous and uncomfortable. What was wrong now?

"Yes, General Sullivan and Colonel Mills asked me to give Sergeant Cliff Ray and you an update about Sergeant Elderhurst and Skye Marlowe. When the team arrived at Harlaxton, they located the manor painting in the soup kettle as you suspected."

"It's wonderful the painting was found."

"I know Mrs. Van der Elst will be pleased to have it returned to the manor."

"Sergeant Elderhust was planning to return to Harlaxton to retrieve the painting, but he was killed before that happened. Of course, you are very familiar with the accident. Have you healed from your injuries?"

"Yes, I have. If I may ask, is the manor painting linked to the D-Day invasion occurring today?"

"I don't have clearance to tell you very much, but yes, it is linked to some landing sites in France. It was fortunate the painting didn't end up in the hands of the Nazis. General Sullivan and Colonel Mills want to thank you both for all your work and personal sacrifices. Also, Ella Cook was informed about how Skye Marlowe used her plane to return to England. There will be some changes made in the procedures within that program."

"Lieutenant, I have one last question about Skye Marlowe. I know she used to work at *The Gregory* and then returned there later. How did Skye get into the United States?"

"After intelligence officers questioned Skye, she broke down and confessed. She was approached by a German agent while she worked at *The Gregory*. The agent offered her a large amount of money to steal the painting. At the time, she was dating Elderhurst and brought him into the scheme to help her. The Germans gave her forged identification to get to the United States. Then, she infiltrated Ella Cook's women aviators by wearing a stolen WAC uniform and hiding in the cargo hold of the plane. I think you know where the story went from there."

"Lieutenant MacGregor, thank you so much for clearing everything up for me. Certainly, Sergeant Cliff Ray will be very interested in hearing this new information as well."

The Conclusion
High Wycombe, England
June - July 1944

Captain Glenn Miller and his band came to perform for the Eighth Army Air Corps troops stationed at High Wycombe, England on July 29, 1944. Later, in the war, Captain Glenn Miller was presumed dead when his plane did not arrive in Paris, France on December 15, 1944.

Chapter 20

It had been a long time since Agnes had seen her parents, brother and sister. She wasn't a teenager, but she missed her family terribly. It would be wonderful to go home soon. How could she tell Cliff her swell news? Would he be happy? Would he want her to stay in England until he was discharged? She saw Cliff walking toward her, and she gave him a huge grin and met him just outside the garden walk. It seemed to be their favorite place to discuss their problems or their joys.

Walking toward Agnes, Cliff couldn't wait to tell her the news. The guys loved to have popular entertainers come to the war zones to cheer the troops. Looking more closely at Agnes, Cliff thought she sure looked happy and had a beautiful glow about her today.

He couldn't wait to tell her the latest news on the base, "Hi, Aggie, I just heard that Glenn Miller and his band is coming here on 29 July to perform for the troops at High Wycombe. It's all the buzz among the guys at the hangar. *Moonlight Serenade* is the band's theme song, you know. It's going to be a swell time for all the guys. I'm sorry you won't be here then."

With her mood slightly dampened, Agnes continued, "Yes, I'll be sad to miss Captain Miller perform, but I'll be busy at home." Thinking she couldn't wait to tell Cliff her news, she went on patiently. Unfortunately, there wasn't enough time to explain everything now.

"Cliff, I have something to tell you! Meet me at 1800 hours near the hangar. I will be finished with dinner clean up, and we can talk then. Will you be finished with today's repairs of the P-47s?"

Even though Cliff seemed confused about what she was trying to say, or not say, he continued, "I don't know, Aggie. I'll have to see how much work the guys and I get done today. The planes are fairly shot up after the last raid. Also, I need to check with my pilots to see what they need before tomorrow's big mission. I'll do my best to get there on time. What's up?" Cliff asked.

Not wanting to tip her hand now, and there was really not enough time to give this secret the attention it deserved, she confidently replied, "I'll tell you this evening. Have a good day. Love you," Agnes replied happily. Agnes walked back to the Mess Hall and pondered what she would say this evening. She truly loved Cliff and wanted his approval. Time would tell how he would take this latest bit of information.

Aggie needed some reflection time before she went to the Mess Hall. Life was always changing, and she would adapt as usual. As she approached the lake, she heard a noise to her left. She was still a little jumpy after all the problems with Elderhurst and Skye. To her delight, she saw Edie Slate looking out at the clear water.

"Hi Edie." Aggie said happy to see her new friend. She was delighted Edie looked so happy today.

"Oh, Aggie, it's so good to see you. You look as if you have a glow about you today. Do you have anything you want to share?"

"Well, I do have some news, but I should tell Cliff first. Tomorrow, come by the Mess Hall, and we will chat over my apple pie and coffee. Why do you look so happy today? Perhaps, it has something to do with a certain young private I see you eating with now."

"Well, I have made a new friend. His name is Howard Tompkins, and he is so easy to talk to. Even though I don't have a lot of free time, I do have to eat."

"That's wonderful news, Edie. Listen I should go get things done at the Mess Hall. See you later – and Private Tompkins."

1800 hours – twilight near the hangars

Coming toward her Cliff gave Agnes a quick wave and a wide smile, "Red, I've been thinking about you all day. I wondered to myself, 'what's she up to now?'"

Cliff and Agnes had been a great team of detectives, but the Case of the Escape Kit had not been solved. No one came forward to claim it – doing so would have opened them up for questioning from their superiors. The pair's subtle questioning around the base turned up no information that anyone was willing to share at least. This mystery would remain – a mystery.

Nervously, Agnes started the conversation and wanted Cliff to guess her news without having to spell it out, "Well, there is a mystery that I solved today." Agnes wanted to stretch this out for a while.

"You mean without me?" Cliff responded wondering where Agnes was going with this puzzle. Usually she came right out with her important information. He thought, I wonder what has happened.

"You are involved that's for sure. Well, you know how I have been sick in the mornings, and I thought it must be the damp English air. I went to the base doctor this morning just to be sure, and it turns out it has nothing to do with the air! You are going to be a papa!" Agnes said proudly.

A huge simile covering his face, he said, "Aggie! Honey, that's great news! I can't wait to write and tell the folks. Oh, how do you feel now? Can I get you something?" Cliff exclaimed excitedly. "My family is going to be so excited that there is going to be a new little Ray running around in a few months. I'll write and tell them, if that's okay with you...or do you want to tell them yourself when you get back to Tennessee?"

"Relax, Cliff. No, you go ahead and write your family that I am being discharged on 7 July and will be coming home. They will be so excited about the baby, I'm sure. "Hey, have you thought of any names for the baby?"

Cliff looked at Agnes hopelessly and replied, "No, Red, you just told me...I haven't had a chance to think of a name...we don't know if it's a boy or a girl. Hey, I may not be able to get home before it's born either. You're a strong gal, and the family will be with you too. Just let me know as soon as he or she has arrived. This is just great!" Cliff said.

Cliff thought this was swell news; with all the bad news about the war, this was wonderful to hear. He couldn't wait to tell Bob, Mac, and all the other mechanics their wonderful, sweet news.

Agnes continued, "I will be leaving for the states soon. I'll miss you so much! Cliff, come back as soon as they let you go. I know the war will be over soon! After all, we are the good guys and the good guys always win! Right!" Agnes said with a tear coursing down her cheek. She couldn't hold in all the emotions that she felt at this moment. Her tears were happy tears though. She sure loved this man!

Cliff smiled at Agnes not sure what to say next. He had never been a father before, "Hey, Red, don't cry! I'm going to miss you terribly! I wish I could buy you some roses or some candy...some gift because of the baby." He gathered her in his arms and gave her a huge kiss and hug. He was going to miss seeing Aggie every day until he could come home too.

"Oh Cliff. You have given me everything I will ever need. Let's solve mysteries together forever!"

Author's Note

Clifton Ray and Agnes Taylor Ray are real people who were high school sweethearts in Red Boiling Springs, Tennessee. They enlisted in the U.S. Army and were both stationed at the base at High Wycombe, England during WWII. Clifton was an airplane mechanic and Agnes was a cook in the military and prepared a meal for General Dwight D. Eisenhower. They were married at High Wycombe and honeymooned at Clovelly, England - probably at the Red Lion Hotel.

This is a historical fiction book, so all the historical events are true, but most of the adventures and secret missions that Cliff and Agnes did were fictional. I have talked to several family members who filled in details about who Clifton and Agnes were and how they may have reacted to these events.

Harlaxton Manor is a castle located in Grantham, England. I do not have any proof that they visited Harlaxton, but it makes a good story! I have visited Harlaxton Manor and researched its history. It is a wonderful manor rich in history and deserves a place in this story. I think that Clifton and Agnes would have enjoyed visiting Harlaxton!

Some characters are also real people. Vera Slaton Nuckols is a U.S. Army veteran and a cook in the military during WWII. William John McDonnel was an WWII airplane mechanic though not in England. Mark Elderhurst was based on an actual soldier who died under mysterious circumstances, but much of his role in the book was fiction. Edie Slate was based on a real person who lived in the South during the 1940's; however, most of her story was fiction, and she was not a real code breaker during the war. Edie knew Agnes and Clifton Ray.

Cubby and Maggie are real people who live in England. Maggie was an evacuee from London during WWII; however, she did not live with Mrs. Clarke who is an imaginary person. Also, Midge Whitethorpe is based on a person living in England.

Best regards,

Linda E. Minton

The Long Gallery

Army cookbook for Mess Hall
cooking. Circa 1942-45

Clifton Ray

Graduation Picture

Agnes Taylor – U.S. Army

18 December 1942 – 7 July 1944

Clifton Delano Ray

U. S. Army – Enlisted 29 November 1941

Agnes and Clifton Ray

Honeymooning at

Clovelly, England

1944

Harlaxton Manor

Grantham, England

Railway Tunnel

Cedar Staircase

The Conservatory

Gregory Windows

Gardner's Cottage

Lion Terrace Garden

The Gregory – Pub

Group Discussion Questions

1. How did WWII affect the everyday life of American couples? How did the war affect some couple's marriage plans?

2. What are some of the character traits of Agnes and Cliff?

3. Brainstorm some traits you consider important about a hero. List some examples from the book.

4. The mystery of the Escape Kit was not solved. Who do you think the "Escape Kit" belonged to?

5. What were the words Agnes heard over and over from Skye and Elderhurst?

6. How did rationing affect families during the war? How did recipes change for many households?

7. Should Agnes and Cliff have told their superiors about the "accidents" which happened?

8. What do letters tell us about relationships, families, and friendships?   Between Agnes and Vera? Between Agnes and her sisters?

9. Discuss the ways communication has changed in the last seventy years. For example, e-mail, letters, phones, television.

10. Explain who the evacuees were in the story, and why they were sent away from the city. How did the bombing of London affect the British children?

Bibliography

Guidebook

Harlaxton Manor, Text by Staff of Harlaxton College, Designed by Jamieson Eley

Books

_____, "Army Food and Messing" The Complete Manual of Mess Management. Compliments of Vera Nuckols U.S. Army veteran and cook. Circa 1941. Accessed December 20, 2018

Manchester, William and Paul Reid, The Last Lion, Little Brown and Company, New York, 2012, p. 353

Pamphlet

Harlaxton College, Beyond Your Imagination, Study Abroad Program, University of Evansville

Magazine

The Evacuee, The Magazine of the Evacuees Reunion Association, Issue 191 November/December 2014

Map

"A Gathering of Eagles – 8th Air Force Style" www.google.com/maps/places/Clovelly, Bideford, UK

Websites

www.americanairmuseum.com/place/173, Accessed September 25, 2018

www.amp.theguardian.com, Monday 12 May 1941, Westminster Abbey hit. Accessed December 17, 2018

www.armywomen.org/songs. Last updated February 2018. Accessed December 12, 2018

www.atomicheritage.org/history/women=army-corps-wac. Last updated April 27, 2018. Accessed May 21, 2019

www.britannica.com/place/Stuttgart-Germany, Accessed January 6, 2019

www.denverpost.com, Forgotten women on the front lines of World War II by Liz Mundy, August 10, 2017, "The Unwomanly Face of War: An Oral History of Women in World War II by Svetlana Alexievich. Accessed January 12, 2019

www.dpcamps.org/stuttgart.html. Accessed January 6, 2019

www.evasioncomete.org, Accessed November 27, 2018, "The Escape and Evasion Materials for Allied Airmen" by Edouard Reniere` - December 2011

www.findagrave.com, Accessed 27 August 2018, memorial page for Agnes Taylor Ray, (27 Jul 1919-13 Aug 2009), Find A Grave Memorial no. 40685968, Gamaliel Cemetery, Gamaliel, Kentucky

www.findagrave.com, accessed 27 August 2018, Clifton Delano Ray, (17 May 1917 - 5 Jul 2013) Memorial no. 113382083, Gamaliel Cemetery, Gamaliel, Kentucky *www.glennmillertrust.co.uk*, AAF Glenn Miller Concert 1944 High Wycombe, England, Captain Glenn Miller's American Band of the AAF. Accessed January 3, 2019

www.harlaxtonmanorarchives.wordpress.com, Harlaxton Manor Archives. Great Hall Window. Accessed October 20, 2018

www.history.com, Dwight D. Eisenhower, Accessed October 20, 2018, Updated August 28, 2018

www.historylearningsite.co.uk, Dwight Eisenhower, C.N. Trueman: Dwight Eisenhower: 20 April 2015. 11 October 2018, Accessed October 20, 2018

www.museumoffloridahistory.com, Accessed October 3, 2018. "The German Submarine Threat off Florida's Coast" and "Military Training in Florida WAAC Training at Daytona Beach" and "Floridians in Military Service: Women on Duty. Military Training in Florida."

www.mylearning.org, Women at War: The Role of Women During WW2, "Taking Over 'Men's" Work, Accessed January 12, 2019

www.nysarchivewomen.weebly.com/wasps-waacs-waves1.htm. Accessed November 5, 2018

www.royalcourt.no, World War II – The Royal House of Norway, 08.01.2007. Accessed June 29, 2019

www.sarahsundin.com, Today in World War II History, posted Tuesday, July 3, 2018 by Sarah Sundin. Accessed March 28, 2019

www.secondworldwarhistory.com, Events of 1944 – WW2 Timeline. Accessed January 12, 2019 www.secure.in.gov/library/2478.htm, ISL: USO in Indpls. Indiana State Library. Accessed July 1, 2019.

www.specialoperations.com, Accessed December 6, 2018, The Eighth Air Force "The Mighty Eighth" Was Born On This Day 1942, by Steve Balestrieri, January 29, 2018.

www.theatlantic.com, "London During the Blitz: Then and Now Photographs," Alan Taylor, May 9, 2016, Accessed December 17, 2018.

www.thehistorypress.co.uk, 'Doing their Bit': The female fighter pilots of WWII, Jacky Hyams. Accessed July 2, 2019

www.theguardian.com, "Children of Wartime Evacuation", Julie Summers 11 March 2011, Accessed February 4, 2019

www.thoughtco.com, A Military Profile of General Dwight D. Eisenhower by Kennedy Hickman. Updated February 28, 2018. Accessed December 8, 2018

www.tracesofwar.com. "Pegasus Memorial – Harlaxton, Accessed December 31, 2018

www.warfarehistorynetwork.com, Voyages to Victory: RMS Queen Mary's War Service. December 13, 2018, Eric Niderost, July 1, 2019

www.worldfacts.us/Dusseldorf.htm, Dusseldorf, Germany – World Facts. Accessed January 6, 2019

www.worldwar2history.info. World War II Timeline 1943. Accessed May 20, 2019

www.worldwar.two.net. World War Two, Barrage Balloons. Accessed January 19, 2019 www.wordpress.com, Pegasus Memorial. Accessed December 31, 2018

www.ww2db.com. Dwight Eisenhower Contributor: C. Peter Chen, Accessed October 20, 2018

Video accounts

St. Agnes, Cornwall – YouTube, uploaded by the St. Agnes Chamber of Commerce, Posted October 15, 2014. Accessed December 15, 2018

Original photographs

Harlaxton Manor, Grantham, England. Permission granted by University of Evansville, Evansville, Indiana.

Military picture of Agnes Taylor, circa 1943, Compliments of son, Charles Ray.

High School Graduation picture, Clifton Ray, 1941 Compliments of Carol Smith.

Honeymoon picture of Clifton and Agnes Taylor Ray, Compliments of Cleo Ray Johnson, February 1944.

First-Hand Accounts and Background Information

1. Willis Deckard - Red Boiling Springs, Tennessee, October 2018. Pictures, backgrounds information, and obituary of both Clifton and Agnes Taylor Ray

2. Glen Eakle - Early family background information on Clifton Ray and Agnes Taylor, October 2018

3. Phil Elder - Military background information October 2018

4. Jill "Cubby" Fox – British WWII evacuee

5. Margaret Galter – British WWII evacuee

6. Cleo Ray Johnson, sister of Clifton Ray, September 2018. Family background information and pictures.

7. Rae MacLeod, British background information on the war and evacuees.

8. David McDonnel and Edie McDonnel – airplane mechanics information. Firsthand accounts of William John "Mac" McDonnel

9. Marion Meier, U.S. Air Force veteran, background information on aircraft, December 28, 2018

10. Vera Nuckols – background information about military cooking and the Mess Hall

11. Charles Ray, son of Agnes and Clifton Ray – background information

12. John Wakelin - British historian, military regulations, and general British information, September 2018

13. Sandra Ray Watkins, daughter of Agnes and Clifton Ray – background information

LINDA E. MINTON, AUTHOR BIO

****

Linda Minton, a retired elementary teacher from Indiana, has an interest in World War II and has written two books, *WWII Heroes & Remembering WWII Women,* on that subject. *The Harlaxton Heist,* her third book which is historical fiction also set during WWII will be published in late summer 2019. Linda is married to husband, Ray, and enjoys traveling and quilting.

****

WWII HEROES: WE WERE JUST DOING OUR JOBS

This is a collection of WWII stories from the European, Pacific, and the China, Burma, India theater of combat. It's important to know what these veterans endured, suffered, and survived. Published 2017.

REMEMBERING WWII WOMEN

This is a collection of the life stories of fifty-five women during the 1940's and how WWII affected their lives. The stories include military, Rosies, Homefront, and ladies from other countries. A common phrase was, "I didn't do anything." They certainly did a lot to help the war effort. Published 2018.

****

THE HARLAXTON HEIST

This story is loosely based on the lives of two real people, Clifton and Agnes Ray. They were in the U.S. Army and based in High Wycombe, England. They rekindle their romance & solve mysteries together. Published 2019.

Linda's books can be found on amazon.com

SPECIAL THANKS

Thanks to Dr. Holly Carter and her staff for their help and encouragement during my research of Harlaxton Manor.

Thanks to the University of Evansville for allowing me to use their campus in England, Harlaxton Manor, in this story.

Thanks to my husband, Ray, for his help and encouragement during my time of travel and compilation of this story.

Thanks to Agnes and Clifton Ray's surviving children Charles Ray and Sandra Watkins for their insights into Agnes and Clifton's life.

Characters not identified as actual people are fictitious. Permission was acquired for descriptions and pictures of Harlaxton Manor, Grantham, England.

11078054R10138

Made in the USA
Monee, IL
08 September 2019